You are cordially invited to…
Honour thy pledge
to the
Miami Confidential Agency

Do you hereby swear to uphold the law to the best of your ability…

To maintain the level of integrity of this agency by your compassion for victims, loyalty to your brothers and sisters and courage under fire…

To hold all information and identities in the strictest confidence…

Or die before breaking the code?

Available in September 2007 from Mills & Boon® Intrigue

Secret Weapon Spouse

BJ DANIELS

MILLS & BOON®
Pure reading pleasure

14294790

First published in Great Britain 2007
by Harlequin Mills & Boon Limited,
Eton House, 18-24 Paradise Road, Richmond, Surrey TW9 1SR

© Harlequin Books S.A. 2006

Special thanks and acknowledgement are given to BJ Daniels for her
contribution to the MIAMI CONFIDENTIAL mini-series.

ISBN: 978 0 263 85749 8

46-0907

Harlequin Mills & Boon policy is to use papers that are
natural, renewable and recyclable products and made from
wood grown in sustainable forests. The logging and
manufacturing processes conform to the legal environmental
regulations of the country of origin.

Printed and bound in Spain
by Litografia Rosés S.A., Barcelona

This book is for fellow writer Marty Levine
who was in my thoughts all the time I was
in Miami. Thanks for adding a ray of
sunshine to those otherwise drab days.

BJ DANIELS's

life dream was to write books. After a career as
an award-winning newspaper journalist, she sold
thirty-seven short stories before she finally wrote
her first book. That book, *Odd Man Out*, received
a 4½ star review from *Romantic Times BOOKclub*
and went on to be nominated for Best Intrigue of
1995. Since then she has won numerous awards,
including a career achievement award for romantic
suspense.

BJ lives in Montana with her husband, Parker, two
springer spaniels, Scout and Spot, and an ageing,
temperamental tomcat named Jeff. When she isn't
writing, she snowboards, camps, boats and plays
tennis. To contact BJ, write to her at PO Box 183,
Bozeman, MT 59771, USA or check out her website
at www.bjdaniels.com.

CAST OF CHARACTERS

Samantha Peters – The wedding planner/undercover agent lived a secret life that even her closest associates didn't know about…until she met a man who saw behind the façade.

Alex Graham – Estranged from his blue-blood family, the fireman never dreamed his sister's wedding would lead to murder.

Caroline Graham – All she wanted was to marry the man she loved – and keep her deadly secrets until the big day.

CB Graham – The patriarch ruled his family with an iron fist. But not even he knew everything.

Brian Graham – Big brother would do anything to look good in his father's eyes.

Preston Wellington III – Caroline's fiancé was one of the few who knew the truth. But he was nowhere to be found.

Sonya Botero – The kidnapped heiress had Miami Confidential working day and night to find her and bring her home safely.

Craig Johnson – Sonya's limo driver wound up in the hospital thanks to some very determined kidnappers. But does he know more than he's letting on?

Victor Constantine – The contract killer had spent years doing what he did so well. Was this his last client?

Miami Confidential – No matter what it takes, the agents who make up this secret, undercover organisation are prepared to fight crime and protect the innocent.

Chapter One

Trouble. Samantha Peters knew it the moment she saw the bride-to-be. Caroline Graham looked upset but trying hard not to show it as she stepped into Samantha's office, followed by a man who was clearly not her fiancé.

"Thank you for making time to see me today," Caroline said, then seemed to remember she wasn't alone. "This is my brother, Alex."

Samantha came around her desk to shake his hand. He was tall, broad in the shoulders with light brown hair—almost blond—and intense eyes that at first she thought were blue but on closer inspection found they changed color with the light. Right now they were more green and flecked with gold.

As her hand disappeared into his large one, she found his touch dry and warm, his grip strong, self-assured. But Samantha wouldn't have expected anything less from one of Caroline Graham's brothers.

Alex, she recalled from her research, was the fireman. In her business, Samantha made a point of knowing as much as she could about her client's family.

As she shook Alex Graham's hand she told herself he could just as easily have been the brother who ran the Graham financial empire instead of the black sheep of the family. He looked completely at home in the expensive pin-striped gray suit that fit him perfectly.

Her eyes locked with his for just an instant. He seemed distracted, his sister Caroline nervous. Samantha couldn't help but wonder why Caroline had called, insisting she had to see her—let alone why she'd brought her brother with her today instead of her fiancé.

"Please sit down," Samantha said as he released her hand. She pushed her tortoiseshell-rimmed glasses up and braced herself for the worst.

She'd been in this business long enough not to jump to conclusions let alone panic. Cool under pressure. That was Samantha Peters. Some said ice water ran through her veins. They had no idea. But if there was one asset she brought to her job as a wedding planner, it was unruffled composure. The same went for her other job—the one that took place in the hidden sound-proof room upstairs over the shop.

At Weddings Your Way, Samantha was the detail person. She was the one who saw that each client's wedding came off without even the tiniest snag. It was one of the reasons she was paid the big bucks.

"Is there a problem?" Samantha asked when Caroline and Alex had taken their chairs. Normally, she would have pulled up a chair, as well, making the meeting more informal, more personal.

Today, Samantha chose to sit behind her desk. That alone should have told her something.

The thing about brides was that they often panicked for all kinds of reasons: family arguments that required a change of setting at both the wedding and reception; the loss or gain of too much weight before their final dress fitting; bridesmaids who got pregnant, broke their legs, cut their hair or dyed it a hideous color before the wedding. The list went on and on.

It was Samantha's job to pacify all parties and solve those problems if possible before the big day. She wasn't too worried even though the Graham-Wellington wedding would be one of the largest affairs Weddings Your Way would handle this year and that was saying a lot given their clientele. Also Samantha had been working on this wedding for more than six months and still had six months to go since Caroline wanted a Christmas wedding and it was only June.

"How can I help you?" she asked looking up from her desk at the bride-to-be. Caroline Graham was tall and willowy, blond and beautiful with a grace born of good genes and unlimited money.

"There might be a problem," Caroline said, fiddling with her engagement ring. Another bad sign.

Alex shifted in the plush chair provided for clients, his gaze lingering on his sister, a frown furrowing his brow.

Samantha could feel the tension in the air, a high-pitched electric inaudible buzz. He looked at Samantha as if he didn't have any more of a clue than she did. She felt an unexpected jolt as he continued to probe her gaze for…for what? She had no idea.

She'd already pulled out the Graham-Wellington file and gone over the details after Caroline's call. But she opened it now and picked up her pen, concentrating on the checklist form in front of her to regain her balance. She had a gift when it came to hysterical brides and grooms with cold feet. She would have taken either right now. There was something about Alex Graham that she found unnerving and clearly Caroline was upset. Her instincts told her this was much more serious than wedding jitters.

"Are there some changes you would like to make?" Samantha asked looking again at the bride-to-be.

"Just one," Caroline said quietly, seeming almost embarrassed. "We'd like to move the wedding up by three months."

To her credit, Samantha didn't even blink. She told herself nothing a bride requested could surprise her at this point in her career. "Three months?"

Caroline explained that her fiancé's father wasn't in good health. They feared that if they waited he might miss the wedding. "It can't be helped under the circumstances."

Samantha flipped to her calendar. The Graham-Wellington wedding was set for the first week in December. For more than six months the date had been set, the plans made, arrangements being prepared. The kind of wedding required for the daughter of one of the wealthiest men in Florida took time. Starting from almost scratch and pulling off something of that magnitude in less than three months was impossible.

"I know it's not much time," Caroline said apologetically.

Samantha glanced at Alex. He was staring at his sister as if this was the first he'd heard of this change. Samantha shifted her gaze to Caroline, saw the set of her jaw and didn't bother to ask if this was something the bride-to-be was sure she wanted to do. Clearly it was.

"All right," Samantha said and flipped through her book. "Do you have a date in mind?"

"The first Friday in September."

September. There went the winter-white dress, the ice-blue bridesmaids dresses, as well. "Were you thinking fall colors then?" she asked calmly.

"I suppose so," Caroline said.

Samantha noted that Caroline's fingers were digging into the fine fabric of her purse now on her lap. She'd never seen the woman nervous before.

The bridesmaids had all been fitted for the dresses that were being made by an impossible-to-get Miami designer. Impossible to get, unless you were Samantha Peters and had the full power of Weddings Your Way behind her.

Maybe they could keep the original wedding dress since there was no way to get another designer original made in three months, not with the designers booked solid. Not even Samantha could pull that off.

But blue was all wrong for a fall wedding this year. That meant new dresses for the twelve bridesmaids. Each would have to be refitted for original designs. Even if Caroline might have agreed to off-the-rack bridesmaid dresses, Samantha doubted C. B. Graham would.

"A fall wedding will be much warmer," Samantha said cheerfully. Fortunately, the wedding was to be held at the Graham estate. So a change of venue wouldn't be required. But that was only the tip of the iceberg. She pulled out a stack of new forms. "What flowers do you have in mind?" Arctic white roses were all wrong for September.

Caroline sighed. "I suppose this changes everything, doesn't it?"

For the type of wedding C. B. Graham had insisted his only daughter have? Yes, this changed everything.

As they began the arduous task again, Samantha made suggestions keeping with what was socially required of a Graham heir. She didn't bother to tell Caroline that the wedding would cost ten times as much—not to mention any money already spent on the first wedding plans was lost. Money, of course, wasn't the issue. Samantha was going to have to call in some favors to pull this one off.

Caroline looked close to tears as she made her selections for a second time. Samantha did her best to make it as painless as possible since Caroline was clearly upset.

Her brother shifted uncomfortably in his chair and said nothing, but Samantha was very aware of him.

She caught him studying his sister from time to time and couldn't help but wonder why Caroline had brought him with her today. For support? He seemed to be as confused by all this as Samantha herself. And where was Preston Wellington III, Caroline's fiancé?

But what worried Samantha was that Caroline's heart didn't seem to be in the choices she was making this time. The bride-to-be seemed more relieved than anything else when the basics has been decided and Samantha walked the two of them to the front door of Weddings Your Way. Caroline looked a little pale and unsteady on her feet as Alex opened the door for her.

"Are you all right?" Samantha heard him say. She didn't catch Caroline's reply as the door closed, but she watched the two of them from the large glass doors as they started down the long flower-and-palm-lined walk to the street. Samantha couldn't shake the feeling that Caroline was anything but all right.

ALEX GRAHAM was thinking the same thing as he and his sister stepped out into the Miami heat, Caroline in the lead.

She's in some kind of trouble.

The thought came out of nowhere and had no real basis. Sure it was unusual that Caroline had changed her wedding date, maybe especially this late. But things happened.

No, what was really odd and unnerving was the fact that she'd called him out of the blue and asked him to meet her at the wedding planner's today. For years he'd been on the outs with his family, Caroline included.

Caroline was the baby girl of his blue-blooded family. It didn't help that their mother had died shortly after she was born. Or that C. B. Graham had tried to make up for it by giving Caroline any and everything she wanted.

Caroline, or the little princess as Alex called her, had been spoiled and difficult. For years he'd avoided her as well as his father and brother, telling himself it was no big loss.

In truth, his family avoided him probably more than the other way around. He'd been the black sheep ever since he refused to attend an Ivy League college—and then had the audacity to become a fireman.

His father, C.B., was an overachiever who swore that the bottom line was always money. Fortunately for C.B., his firstborn, Brian, had followed in his footsteps attending the old man's alma mater and going into the family investments business.

C.B. had almost disowned Alex when he'd gone to a state college and then become a Miami fireman. Needless to say, they still didn't get along. In fact, his father had nothing but contempt for Alex's choices and did little to hide it.

"Caroline?" Alex called after his sister as she walked ahead of him. The afternoon sun hung over the brightly painted buildings along the street, the day uncomfortably hot and humid. It was only June. He hated to think what August would be like. Palm fronds rustled in the hot breeze off Biscayne Bay. Somewhere in the distance came the screech of tires, the blare of a horn. Had she not heard him?

"Caroline?" She'd said little since he'd met her here and he wasn't going to let her get away until they talked. Really talked, something his family avoided at all costs.

She'd stopped and seemed to be leaning against a wrought-iron bench as if she felt ill.

Alex caught up to his sister and saw that she was flushed and appeared close to tears. He took her arm. "Hey, are you all right? You don't look so good. What's going on?"

He couldn't shake the feeling that his sister asked him here today to confide something in him—and changed her mind.

"I told you, I'm fine," she snapped, pulling free. "I just need to get to the car and sit down for a minute. The heat." She blew out a breath and fanned herself, stepping away to head for her car and driver waiting at the curb. "I'll call you later," she said over her shoulder, her pace increasing as if she couldn't wait to get away from him. "Thank you for meeting me here."

Alex swore under his breath, wondering what he'd done. Nothing. They hadn't even spoken two words from the time he'd met her in the Weddings Your Way lobby. It wasn't him this time, he told himself. She was upset about something else. Being forced to change the date of the wedding?

He saw her look around as if she'd been expecting someone. Her fiancé?

Where was he anyway? Why hadn't he met Caroline here? Alex had the feeling she'd been expecting him. Maybe that's what had her upset—the fact that he hadn't showed.

Alex had yet to meet his sister's soon-to-be-husband but he already disliked him based simply on the man's name: Preston Wellington III. He, no doubt, was a clone of their brother, Brian, which meant that once Caroline married him she would be spending most of her life never seeing him. Just as they had hardly ever seen their father. He was always too busy making more money to spend any time with them. Alex couldn't bear to think what his sister's life would be like. He'd wanted more for her.

He sighed and started after her, hoping he could change her mind about leaving. Maybe they could go somewhere, have a cool drink, talk.

Out of the corner of his eye, he noticed a white limo pull up to the curb behind his sister's car. He slowed, thinking it was probably the missing Preston Wellington III.

The driver got out to open the rear door. An attractive dark-haired young woman stepped out onto the curb. Caroline had stopped as if she also thought the limo contained someone she knew.

And then everything happened too fast. At first Alex heard rather than saw the commotion that ensued. He turned as a black limo pulled up behind the white one.

Two men leaped from the rear doors. They grabbed the woman who'd just exited the limo in front of them. Her driver tried to fight them off but was knocked to the ground as they dragged the woman to the open doors of the black limo.

Alex charged across the lawn toward the two men who'd shoved the woman into the backseat of the waiting black limo and jumped in after her. The limo engine roared, then to Alex's horror, the large black car jumped the curb as if aiming directly for the woman's limo driver who was still on the ground.

The driver managed to roll out of the way as the limo shot toward Alex. He yelled to Caroline as he dived aside, hitting the ground and rolling, coming up in time to see that the speeding car had turned and was aimed directly at his sister.

Caroline seemed frozen to the spot. He let out a howl of anguish as he heard the limo hit her, her body flying off to the side.

The dark limo had no rear license plate and the windows were too tinted to see inside as it crashed between two cars at the curb and sped off down the street. Everything had happened so fast, he didn't even get a good look at the two men who'd taken the woman.

"Caroline. Oh God, Caroline." Alex was on his feet, running to where she was slumped on the grass. He dropped to the ground next to his sister and felt for a pulse with one hand as he fumbled out his cell phone and dialed 911 with the other. "Oh, Caroline," he whispered as he brushed her hair back from her beautiful face.

He felt a hand on his shoulder but it wasn't until later that he recalled the feel of the woman's touch, let alone remembered her name. Samantha Peters.

INSIDE THE SPEEDING black limo, the man in the back made the call. "We've got the girl," he said when the phone was picked up at the other end.

There was no reply. Just a soft click. In the backseat Sonya Botero's eyes fluttered.

"Give her more of the drug," the man ordered. "I don't want her waking up."

He leaned back and closed his eyes. The job hadn't come off as clean as he'd planned. Unfortunately, he'd left loose ends, he thought glancing back.

CRAIG JOHNSON SAT on the grass in front of Weddings Your Way and watched the black limo disappear down the street, tires squealing and engine roaring.

The limo driver-bodyguard was too shocked to move. The blow to his head had left him dazed but not so dazed that he didn't realize what had just happened.

The men had taken the woman he'd been hired to protect and there would be hell to pay.

But what was utmost in his mind was one startling realization: the men had tried to *kill* him. If he hadn't rolled out of the way when he had…

Suddenly he couldn't catch his breath at just the

thought of how close it had been. He gasped, the weight of the knowledge like a weight on his chest.

He was glad that no one was paying any attention to him now. They'd all crowded around a woman on the ground a dozen yards from him and he realized that unlike him, she'd been hit by the car.

He felt light-headed, his stomach weak and queasy. That could be him over there on the ground.

He tried to get up but his legs wouldn't hold him. Sitting back down heavily on the ground, he watched people rushing around, calling for help. More people were running over. He heard voices above him asking if he was all right. Did he need an ambulance?

He was shaking so hard he couldn't answer. He closed his eyes and lay back on the ground, lucky to be alive. But for how long?

Chapter Two

Samantha Peters pushed her tortoiseshell-rimmed glasses up as she sat at her usual spot at the table in the soundproof room on the second floor of Weddings Your Way, watching the monitors on the wall.

The police had left hours ago. Now the only illumination came from the security lights that bathed the long palm-lined entry into the shop.

Weddings Your Way had been in an uproar all afternoon and evening. No one could believe that Sonya Botero had been abducted right out front and client Caroline Graham had been injured in the hit-and-run that followed.

"We are prepared for a ransom demand," Rachel Brennan was saying now to the elite group of undercover agents positioned around the table. "Everything is in place. Since the abduction took place here, the kidnappers might contact us first. If it *is* a kidnapping."

Samantha found herself only half listening as she

watched the monitors that provided surveillance. She focused on the two that covered the front of the building.

"I've heard from Sonya's father as well as her fiancé," Rachel was saying. "Both are flying in tomorrow. Both will demand answers. Let's do our best to have some for them."

The air conditioner hummed in the large room devoid of windows. One end was a wall of computers and electronics. This was the command center, the heart of the true operation with Weddings Your Way being the front. Not that each agent didn't perform wedding-related duties, living and working in the community while working undercover as part of the Miami Confidential team.

Rachel Brennan, tall, ebony-haired with sparkling blue eyes, in her early forties, was head of the elite group.

"I've looked at the surveillance tapes," Rachel said. "The men knew about the cameras. They were careful to keep their heads down, faces in shadow. It was all very well planned and executed. We can't rule out that Sonya's abduction is connected with the recent assassination attempt on her fiancé."

"So are we assuming this is politically motivated?" Sophie Brooks asked. Sophie, tall, willowy with long blond hair, had been sketching on a pad in front of her and now looked up. Along with being an agent, she was also Weddings Your Way's invitation designer.

"It *has* to be connected to politics," Julia Garcia said in a quiet voice at the end of the table. Julia was friends with Sonya when they were young and now worked as a seamstress for the wedding shop along with being an agent. "When you're about to marry a politician from Ladera who has been making war on drug dealers throughout South America, you can't help but be a target."

The room fell silent for a long moment. Samantha continued to watch the monitors, the tragic events of the day weighing heavily on her. She knew what she was waiting for. Her instincts told her it wouldn't be long now.

"Any word on the condition of Caroline Graham?" Isabelle Rush asked. The agent was small with shoulder-length strawberry blond hair and light brown eyes. She'd been handpicked for the Miami Confidential team as an expert in criminology.

"Still unconscious," Samantha said without looking from the monitors. "The doctors aren't sure she's going to make it."

"Is it possible she was a target, as well?" Isabelle asked.

Samantha recalled how the car had careened up onto the curb, just missing the limo driver and Alex Graham but hitting Caroline. "I don't see how. Caroline didn't even have an appointment. I had to fit her in at the last minute so no one could have known she was coming here."

"Maybe," Rachel said and turned to Clare Myers, who was sitting at one of the computers. "Let's not take any chances. Find out everything you can on both. Did Sonya and Caroline know each other? I want to know if there is even the remotest connection between them."

"I'm on it," Clare said tapping at the keys. The small

pixie-ish blond woman had a sharp mind and worked for the IRS investigating corporations trying to rip off the government before she was enlisted by Miami Confidential to work as the accountant for the wedding shop as well as use her expertise on digging up anything on anyone via the computer.

"What about Botero's limo driver?" Rachel asked, checking her notes. "Craig Johnson?"

"He was admitted to the hospital complaining of headaches," Isabelle said. "The police questioned him after he was admitted. Johnson said he didn't remember anything after being struck on the head by one of the men."

"Could be lying," Julia said. "But it also could have happened so fast he really didn't get a good look at his attacker."

Isabelle shook her head. "I think one of us should go by and see how he's doing, see what our take on Mr. Johnson is. After all, he was hired as Sonya's bodyguard as well as her driver."

"I'll pay him a visit," Samantha said. "I want to go to the hospital and check on Caroline Graham anyway."

Rachel nodded her approval. "I'm sure the police questioned Caroline's brother. Alex, right?"

Samantha nodded and looked to Isabelle.

"He told police he only got a glimpse of the men," Isabelle said. "The car had no plates on the back and tinted windows."

"Check limo rentals," Rachel said. "It's a long shot."

"I saw the car," Samantha said and felt everyone look toward her again. "I saw some of the incident from the window after I walked Caroline and Alex to the door. You're right. It happened so fast there wasn't anything anyone could have done. I got a good look at the limo, though. It was an older model. Definitely not a rental. You might want to check used car lots."

Rachel gave her a smile. "Good idea." She looked toward Clare who said, "I'm already on it."

Samantha saw movement on the monitors. Just as she'd been expecting, a dark figure started to bang on the door, then saw the receptionist Samantha had asked to stay late. He shoved his way through the front door and into the reception area.

Samantha stood. "Excuse me, but Alex Graham is here. I need to take care of this."

As a former agent and profiler for the FBI, Samantha was the go-to person. Not only did she make sure every wedding went off without a hitch, as an agent she assisted in investigations by noticing the little things about people and cases.

As she rose to leave, everyone's attention turned to the monitor, the same one that had recorded Alex Graham's entrance earlier today. Only now Alex was dressed in jeans, a Miami Fire Department T-shirt that stretched across his broad shoulders and running shoes. His light brown hair curled at the nape of his suntanned neck and looked as if he'd just come from a hasty shower.

"At this point, I don't think it would be wise to assume that Caroline Graham was just an innocent victim," Rachel said. "Find out everything you can about her. And her brother," she said frowning at the monitor screen. "It might not be a coincidence that the two of them just happened to be here at the same time Sonya Botero was abducted."

Samantha nodded and slipped out. She'd known Alex Graham would be back. And she knew even before she'd seen him storm in what he would want.

As she descended the stairs, she caught the scent of him before he saw her. Some kind of masculine-smelling shampoo. Fresh from a quick shower, just as she'd suspected. She noted that his hazel eyes were red rimmed and he looked as if he'd been to hell and back. As she neared him, she felt anguish coming off him as well as a raw angry energy. She braced herself.

Alex Graham looked up as she came down the stairs to meet him. His eyes locked with hers and she thought she glimpsed relief. "I wasn't sure you'd still be here."

"Mr. Graham, why don't we step into my office?" Samantha said in her all-business voice.

He gave a sharp nod and stalked ahead of her into her office. She closed the door behind them and took her place behind the desk.

"How is your sister?" she asked, although she'd called the hospital not long before.

"Still unconscious," he said his voice hoarse.

To think that he'd sat in that same chair with his

sister beside him only hours before. Except then he'd been ill at ease, nervous.

Now Alex Graham was grieving and angry. "What the hell happened here today?" he demanded.

"You know as much as I do," Samantha said quietly as she adjusted her glasses.

"I highly doubt that. Who was that woman in the limo?"

"One of our clients," Samantha said. "I'm afraid I can't tell you her name because the police have instructed us not to."

A muscle in his jaw bunched. He was furious and looking for someone to blame for his sister's accident, but also looking for answers. Samantha wished she had some for him.

"I'm already getting the same runaround from the police, I don't need it from you," he said, his voice rising. "I want to know why my sister was run down outside your business."

She nodded and spoke in the same soothing tone she used with jittery brides-to-be. "We want to know the same thing, Mr. Graham."

"Alex. Mr. Graham is my father." He raked his fingers through his already tousled hair. "My sister may not make it." His voice broke. "I can't reach her fiancé. You know a hell of a lot more than I do. Are you going to help me or not?"

She felt a shiver as she glimpsed the raw pain in his gaze. This man was angry and hurting but he was no fool. He wasn't going to be put off by sympathy and reassuring words. Maybe the hit-and-run had just been an unfortunate accident. But what if for some reason Caroline Graham *had* been a target?

"I'm going to help you."

ALEX GRAHAM leaned back in the chair, all his anger spent. He needed to calm down, to sleep, to eat, but more importantly he needed answers. "Thank you."

She nodded and he found himself settling down a little. She had that kind of effect on people, he thought, remembering how she was with Caroline earlier that day.

He studied her, trying to put his finger on what it was about her that bothered him. She was rail-thin, with huge brown eyes and straight brown hair that fell almost to her shoulders. She peered at him through tortoiseshell glasses. A quiet, unassuming woman, the kind who blended in with the wallpaper.

At least that's what she wanted him to believe.

Where had that thought come from? He met her steady gaze and felt both sympathy and compassion and true concern. And yet as he looked into her eyes, he had the distinct impression that there was more to her, something she didn't want him to see.

"How can I help you?" she asked.

He took a breath. "Let me be honest with you, Miss Peters. It is Miss, right?" Was there a slight flush under the cool porcelain of her skin? "I have never met Caroline's fiancé and quite frankly, I don't even know how to reach him."

"I have a number for him," she said taking a fabric-covered book from her desk drawer. From where he sat, he could see that the contents of the drawer were as neat as the writing in the book.

He watched her turn right to the page.

"Preston Wellington III," she said picking up a pen and printing the number on a Post-it in the same concise handwriting. She tore off the note and handed it to him, closing the book and crossing her arms over it.

He stared at the number for a moment, then at her. "You already tried to call him, didn't you?"

"Yes."

"And you weren't able to reach him."

"I'm afraid not."

He nodded, suspecting he wasn't going to get much help here, either. "And this is the only number you have for him, right?"

"Yes."

"I've tried it, as well, with the same results." He sighed. "Have you met him?"

She nodded. "He always came with Caroline for her appointments."

"Except today?" he asked, sounding surprised.

"Yes."

"And your impression of him?" He saw her hesitate. "I realize I'm putting you on the spot here, but I need to know what I'm up against. I'm worried sick about my sister. Don't you think it was more than odd that the only day her fiancé didn't come with her she changed her wedding plans and then was struck down out front?" He saw something in her eyes that confirmed she, too, thought it odd. "Now no one seems to be able to reach him…. I need to know your impression of him."

She nodded slowly. "I liked him. He seemed very nice, very attentive to your sister. I felt the two of them were very much in love, they seemed to be…soul mates."

He heard the small catch in her throat, not sure what surprised him more—her obvious emotional reaction to witnessing what she'd thought was true love or that his sister and this Wellington III might really share something real.

Was it possible he was wrong about the guy? "Would you mind trying the number again for me?" Maybe they would get lucky.

"Certainly." She picked up the phone and dialed the number from memory, then handed him the phone.

With each ring, his uneasiness grew. He got Preston's voice mail again but didn't leave another message. He handed the phone back to her. "He hasn't returned any of my calls or contacted the hospital. Don't you think that's odd?"

She didn't comment.

He raked a hand through his hair in frustration. What was he doing here? What had made him think this wedding planner could help him? Maybe she really didn't know any more than he did.

But she had met Preston Wellington III, she'd

thought the man was in love with Caroline. Then again, maybe she thought all her clients were in love. Maybe the woman was a hopeless romantic.

He looked into her brown eyes, eyes the color of Cognac. But behind all that rich, warmth was something steely. This woman was no hopeless romantic. There was intelligence there and something else—a wariness that made him wonder if she knew a whole lot more that she wasn't telling him.

"I found another number for Wellington in Caroline's purse and called it," he said, watching for her reaction. "It was his office supposedly. I was told he was out of the country and couldn't be reached. Apparently they don't know when he'll be back." He saw surprise and something else register in her expression: doubt. Finally.

He felt relieved, needing someone else to confirm that his fears might be justified. He recalled the feel of her hand on his shoulder earlier today when he'd been kneeling over his sister's body.

"Thanks, Miss… Could I possibly call you something besides, Miss Peters?"

She seemed to hesitate. "Samantha."

"Thank you." One barrier down, he thought studying her. He couldn't shake the feeling that she was hiding something from him. If it had anything to do with his sister's hit-and-run, he would find out what it was. One way or another. "Samantha, if you're serious about helping me, then you will come with me now."

"COME WITH YOU?" Samantha hadn't been able to hide her surprise. He'd caught her off guard. She'd known he would come back tonight. He was the kind of man who would demand answers and not give up until he got them.

But she worked behind the scenes at Weddings Your Way as an agent. And that's the way she liked it.

"Go where?" she asked.

"I have the keys to my sister's condo and I found what I believe is her new address," he said, sounding almost embarrassed. Obviously he hadn't known where his sister now lived.

He sighed and leaned forward, elbows on his knees as he scrubbed his hands over his face. "I can't go over there by myself."

Samantha swallowed, hearing again the raw pain in his voice, and had she been closer she would have placed a hand on his arm and tried to reassure him. But this wasn't some groom having second thoughts. This was a man whose sister was lying unconscious in a hospital room, possibly dying, a man who was more than a little suspicious not only of Weddings Your Way and why his sister's accident had happened out front—but of Samantha Peters as well.

Samantha had shielded herself from this kind of pain, this kind of intimacy. It was why, after completing her training with the FBI she'd taken the job Rachel had offered her. Samantha wanted to work behind the scene. She didn't want to get close to the victims—let alone the killers.

"I know what I'm asking is an imposition," Alex said not looking at her. "But I can't face it alone. I think Preston has been living with her," he continued before she could say anything. "There might be some clue as to where he is at Caroline's place. Or a number or address that would give me an idea how to reach his family. Something."

"Caroline's friends don't know?" The moment she asked, she realized how foolish the question had been.

He raised his head and met her gaze. "Frankly, I don't know any of her friends. Before yesterday, I hadn't seen Caroline in months."

"And the rest of your family couldn't help?"

His smile held no humor. "My father thinks my concern is premature. He insists that he has left a message for Preston and expects to hear from him soon. He's convinced there is no problem."

"Maybe that's the case."

But clearly Alex didn't believe it. Samantha had to admit she was starting to have doubts, as well. It had been hours since the accident. Preston should have checked his messages and called by now.

"You think something has happened to him?" she asked. She'd feared Sonya's abduction was much bigger in scope than any of them suspected.

"That's just it, I don't know what to think," Alex said. "You saw my sister earlier today. She seem upset to you?" He nodded as if he already knew the answer.

"Something was wrong," he continued. "And I haven't the slightest idea what it was. All I know is that my sister asked me to meet her here today. So where was her fiancé? My sister is fighting for her life and needs him and yet no one can reach him. Don't tell me that doesn't make you wonder. I have to find this Preston Wellington III and satisfy myself that this guy is on the up-and-up." He rose to his feet.

She had no choice but to go with him even though every instinct told her to watch herself closely. She'd seen the way Alex had been studying her. He was suspicious. Which was only natural under the circumstances.

But she had reason to be suspicious of him as well. All she had was his word that Caroline had told him to meet her here today.

Even if Alex Graham was telling the truth, he unnerved her, threw her off balance and made her feel exposed. And that made him dangerous. She would have to be very careful around him.

She pushed out of her chair and reached for her purse, remembering that her gun wasn't in it. "Just give me a minute."

Chapter Three

Samantha was seldom surprised by a man. But Alex, she realized, could turn out to be the exception. He led her to an older model pickup parked at the curb. That didn't surprise her as much as the music that came on when he started the truck.

Country western. He grinned and turned it down. "I'm a big Willie Nelson fan," he said almost apologetically.

There was something so refreshing about Alex—and at the same time, she didn't dare relax around him. Her instincts told her he was trying to get her to lower her guard around him. And she had to wonder why.

The cab of the pickup felt too confined, too intimate. And she was too acutely aware of the man behind the wheel.

Alex, though, seemed relaxed as if relieved to have her with him. Because he thought she was doing this out of the kindness of her heart? Or like her, did he have his own agenda?

She hadn't been paying much attention to where he was driving. He had large hands and he held the wheel like a man who enjoyed driving and drove well.

It wasn't until he pulled to the curb and let out an oath that she looked around.

He had stopped in front of an old five-story building on the edge of an area of the city that had gone to seed long ago. "This can't be right," he said handing the address to Samantha.

"It's the address you have written here," she said, equally surprised. The neighborhood had a deserted feel to it and had for blocks. "It looks like some sort of renewal project."

"My sister can't possibly live here."

A set of headlights flashed behind them, followed by the single whoop of a siren and the flash of blue from a light bar. Samantha looked in her rearview mirror as a patrol car pulled up behind them. Not a cop car but a private security company.

"I'll handle this," Alex said and climbed out to walk back as a uniformed man exited the patrol car.

"Wait—" But her words were lost as the door closed. She picked up her purse from the floorboard, slipping her hand in to close her fingers around the grip of the gun she'd brought as she watched the two in the side mirror.

She waited, reading their body language, one hand on the gun, the other on the door handle. She didn't like the looks of the neighborhood and she knew some of the types who filled security cop openings. This one was late middle age, Hispanic and looked harmless enough.

She saw the security guard point in the direction of the building with the address Alex had found for Caroline.

A moment later, Alex started toward her. The guard climbed back into his patrol car, but didn't leave.

She released her hold on the gun and put her purse back down as Alex opened his door and leaned in.

"You're right about this being a renewal project," he said. "It seems my sister owns it and is its first resident. She lives on the top floor of this building."

He looked as skeptical as Samantha felt. Why would Caroline Graham live here when she could afford to live anywhere? There had to be a mistake.

Alex shut the car door and came around to open hers. As she got out, she looked back at the security guard still sitting in his car behind them. She could see his face under the streetlight and she knew he could see hers, as well.

She gave him a small smile and a nod. The guard would remember her if she needed to come back here.

Alex used one of the keys on the ring he said he'd found in his sister's purse at the hospital and braved the elevator although it appeared to be new and in good condition. It hummed up to the fifth floor and opened.

"What the hell?" Alex said beside her.

Samantha was equally surprised to find the hallway under construction. The location was questionable although she suspected it would have a great view of the Atlantic and was on the edge of an area that was obviously seeing some positive changes. But this place didn't appear to be finished.

"I don't believe this." Alex shook his head and didn't step out of the elevator for a moment as if only more convinced he had the wrong place. "Caroline can't be *living* here."

Apparently she was. At least according to the address Alex had found. And what the security guard had told him.

"Seems to be undergoing a renovation," Samantha said following him as he finally stepped off the elevator into the unfinished hallway.

He shot her a disbelieving look. "The Caroline I know—or knew anyway—wouldn't be caught dead living under these kinds of conditions." He realized what he'd said and grimaced. "It's just that she's always demanded the best that money could buy and had enough money that she never had to compromise."

"I'm sure there is an explanation," Samantha said as she watched Alex try several keys before the knob turned and the door swung open.

From what she could see, most of the condo was walled off behind large sheets of plastic with work being done behind them. "Maybe she saw it as a good investment. Investing does run in your family, right?"

Alex shot her a smile. "If you're trying to make me feel better, it's working."

She pushed aside a corner of the plastic into what was the living room and adjoining kitchen. There was new Sheetrock on the walls and new tile on the counters and backsplash in the kitchen. But the cupboards were still missing and there was Sheetrock dust everywhere.

In fact, Samantha could see tracks in the thick white dust on the floor. Alex might be feeling better about all this, but she wasn't.

Something was wrong here. She just didn't know what yet.

She followed Alex as he pushed aside another plastic area and opened a door on the right. The master suite and bath—and obviously the first rooms completed because it appeared someone had been living in there. There was carpet on the floor, the rooms were furnished and several items of discarded clothing lay across the foot of the crumpled sheets and duvet on the large unmade bed.

Samantha spotted two champagne glasses and an empty bottle on one of the nightstands. She itched to collect both for prints but couldn't in front of Alex without making him suspicious. Wedding planners usually didn't run fingerprints as a sideline.

She would have to come back for them.

ALEX HAD HOPED he'd find something in his sister's condo that would convince him he had nothing to worry about when it came to his sister's fiancé. But coming here had done just the opposite.

What the hell was going on with Caroline?

"Well, this was a mistake," he said and noticed the way Samantha moved to the closet but was careful not to touch anything as if this was a crime scene.

Is that what she suspected? he wondered with a jolt. That Caroline's hit-and-run wasn't an accident?

She seemed to scan the clothing inside as if looking for something in particular.

"I'm telling you my sister can't be staying here," he said. "Look, when I asked my father, he said that she was in the process of moving and had most of her stuff stored at the house."

"Isn't this her clothing?"

He glanced into the closet. While the walk-in closet wasn't overflowing with clothing so it couldn't be Caroline's—at least not yet—there were enough items to make it clear that someone had been staying here.

That's when he noticed a purse on the top shelf with an odd-print scarf tied to the strap.

"That's hers," he said. "I saw her with it one day uptown." He didn't mention that he'd ducked in a store to avoid talking to her. It had to be hers. He remembered the unusual scarf.

"I smell her perfume on some of the clothing," Samantha said from inside the closet. "I also recognize one of the dresses she wore at an appointment I had with her."

Her movements were slow, purposeful. He found himself watching her rather than looking for evidence of Preston Wellington III in the condo.

At first glance, Samantha Peters wasn't the type of woman a man would even notice. Hell, he wouldn't have given her a second glance under other circumstances. It was the way she dressed, he realized with a jolt.

Not that he knew anything about women's clothing, but even he could see that the suit she wore was too large for her slim, small frame, the cut all wrong. She wore it like armor, as if protecting herself, he thought with surprise.

And her hair. It was colored too dark for her pale skin and cut shoulder length, long enough that it often covered part of her face.

And those tortoiseshell glasses. The frames took away from the gold in her brown eyes.

He frowned, wondering why she dressed like that. The woman was too savvy for it to be anything but a calculated choice. Almost as if she was hiding from something, he thought, even more intrigued.

He realized she was looking intently at one of the men's shirts hanging in the closet. "What is it?"

She let go of the sleeve. "Nothing."

Like hell. As she came out, he slipped past her to reach for the shirt, wondering what she wasn't telling him. Was she trying to protect him? Why else wouldn't she tell him?

One glance at the shirt and he saw it was old, looked more like it might belong to one of the construction workers. "Her fiancé left behind only his old clothes, nothing he would bother to come back for. Is that it?"

She turned from where she had stopped midway into the room. "None of this proves anything."

"You still want to believe this guy really loves my

sister and isn't just using her, don't you? I admire your optimism," he said as he joined her in the middle of the large room. "I guess optimism is something you have to have in your line of work given the divorce rate, but I've got to tell you, I don't like any of this." He glanced around the room. "What the hell is Caroline doing here? You've seen her more than I have the last six months. Doesn't this strike you as odd?"

Samantha seemed to hesitate. "A little. Maybe."

He looked at her and shook his head, unable not to smile. He actually did admire her for holding out hope that Preston Wellington III was a good guy with good intentions.

"Earlier today I had the feeling that Caroline wanted to tell me something and that's why she asked me to meet her at your office."

"You had no idea what it was?" she asked.

He shook his head. "But I can think of only one reason my sister would be living like this. She's broke. What if her fiancé has taken all of her money and skipped out on her and that's what she was going to tell me today?"

Samantha frowned. "But why go to the trouble of moving the wedding up three months if that's the case?"

"Hell, I don't know. Maybe she thought she could save the relationship by getting him to the altar sooner."

"Wouldn't she just elope if that were the case?"

He laughed at that. "My father would cut her off without a cent of her inheritance if she did. No, she has to go through with the big wedding. It's required of the only daughter of C. B. Graham and she knows that."

"They were celebrating *something*," Samantha said as she nodded toward an empty champagne bottle and two glasses on a nightstand beside the bed.

He'd been so upset over everything he hadn't even noticed them until now. What would Caroline and Preston have had to celebrate? "He was probably just saying goodbye and she didn't know it," Alex said as he moved closer, noticing the lipstick on the rim of one glass and feeling a horrible sinking feeling as he imagined maybe one of his sister's last happy moments.

That's when he saw it.

He let out a curse.

"Nonalcoholic champagne?" Turning, he stalked into the bathroom where he found what he was looking for in the small wastebasket beside the commode.

"Holy hell, Caroline's *pregnant*," he said as he came out of the bathroom and saw Samantha Peters's expression.

She didn't look the least bit surprised and he realized she'd already figured it out and was way ahead of him.

Hell, he had the feeling she was way ahead of him on a lot of things.

SAMANTHA SAW ALL THE COLOR suddenly drain from Alex's face.

He grabbed for his cell phone, panic in his expression. "*No!* The accident today." He hurriedly tapped in a set of numbers. "Oh, no."

Samantha went into the unfinished living room while he called the hospital. She stepped through a break in the plastic and opened one of the windows, needing fresh air as she said a short prayer for Caroline's baby.

She caught movement from the dark shadows of a building across the street. Someone had been standing there looking up at Caroline's building. The security guard? She couldn't be sure. But why wouldn't he just wait in his car on the street? Unless he needed to relieve himself and couldn't leave the area until his shift was over.

Behind her she heard the rustle of plastic and said another silent prayer before turning. Alex pulled aside the plastic and stepped through into the dimly lit unfinished room.

She held her breath, afraid.

The confirmation of a pregnancy explained a lot— the change in the wedding plans, the way Caroline had looked yesterday, pale and shaky in Samantha's office— and, unfortunately, possibly the missing fiancé.

"I just talked to the doctor. The baby's okay," he said, breathless and scared but looking relieved."

Samantha released the breath she'd been holding and smiled at him, surprised by the tears that misted her eyes. "I'm so glad."

He nodded and pushed aside the plastic again so they could step back into the bedroom out of the construction area. She watched him move to the middle of the room, his back to her, as if he didn't know where to go or what to do next. She knew the feeling.

After a moment, he faced her again and she saw that he was angry. "You *knew* she was pregnant."

"I suspected," she admitted. "She wouldn't be the first bride to move her wedding up because of a pregnancy."

His expression softened. "Sorry. I just feel like everyone is keeping things from me, you know?"

She knew.

He raked his hand through his hair, making him look all that much more vulnerable—and irresistible.

The stab of desire took her by surprise. Her first in a long, long time. She smothered it the way she would have a flickering candle. But unlike a candle flame, this still burned, a slow smoldering burn inside her that never let her quite forget.

"I have to admit, when she moved the wedding up three months, I *did* wonder," he said and lowered himself onto the edge of the bed, then seemed to think better of it and shot back up. "Come on, let's get out of here."

She glanced back at the champagne glasses and bottle. She would come back. It would be fairly easy given that there was no security system installed in the condo yet and she'd made a point of letting the security guard see her— not that she planned to get caught when she returned.

Looking up, she felt a jolt as she saw that Alex Graham was watching her, frowning slightly—almost as if he could see beneath her oversize suits, the glasses, the dyed hair to the woman she tried so hard to hide.

Chapter Four

Alex seemed lost in thought as they left the condo—making her even more convinced he was on to her.

As she slid behind the wheel of the pickup, he looked over at her, his eyes narrowing. His expression changed so quickly, he caught her off guard. "I'm starved. I know you haven't had dinner because I've been dragging you all over Miami." He smiled, bathing her in soft warmth.

Food was the last thing she'd have expected he would want right now. She looked away for a moment, trying to come up with a good excuse and regain her balance.

"I know this great little Mexican food place," he was saying, his enthusiasm growing. "Lupita makes a chile verde that is to die for. Fresh homemade tortillas. And the best margaritas in Southern Florida. Tell me you like Mexican food," he said starting the engine.

She didn't have the heart to tell him that she avoided spicy food. It didn't go with her wedding planner persona. But his enthusiasm was contagious. "Who doesn't like Mexican food?" she said, smiling as she turned back to him.

He gave her one of his heart-stopping smiles. "You should do that more often," he said, suddenly serious again.

"What?" She hadn't realized she'd done anything.

"Smile. It looks good on you."

She ducked her head, embarrassed by the way she felt when Alex Graham looked at her like that. It was as if he could see behind the facade. That he could see *her*. The real her. And if that was true, then she was in big trouble.

As he drove toward the café, she looked out her side window, trying to get her feet back under her. Alex Graham was like a whirlwind. He caught you up, taking you places you never expected to go, promising the wildest ride of your life. But she knew that eventually he'd let her down. Men always did. And the drop back to reality this time would be a killer.

Something caught her eye in her side mirror. She'd seen that car earlier when they'd left Weddings Your Way. One of the headlights had a different bulb in it giving the car the appearance of winking.

The car was staying back, changing lanes, even disappearing for short periods of time. Whoever was driving knew what he was doing.

As Alex pulled into the dark parking lot next to the café, Samantha saw the nondescript tan car drive past. She only got a glimpse of the man behind the wheel, his face in shadow.

"You all right?" Alex asked.

"Sorry, just daydreaming," she said with a shrug.

He nodded, but she could tell that he'd seen her reaction when she'd realized they were being followed. He didn't seem to miss much but he let it go as he insisted on opening her door as if they were on a date.

The café was small and quiet no doubt because it was late and a weekday night. Samantha excused herself to freshen up. In the empty ladies' room, she used her cell phone to call Rachel.

In as few words as possible, Samantha filled her in.

Rachel let out a low whistle when Samantha finished. "You're sure Preston was the man who shared the champagne with Caroline in her condo?"

"No. But I smelled his aftershave. He'd been in the condo recently. That doesn't mean there isn't another man."

"What's bothering you?" Rachel asked. "I hear it in your voice."

Rachel knew her too well. Samantha glanced at her watch. She had to get back to Alex before he began to worry—and wonder. "The men's clothing in the closet. It's all wrong." She explained that the shirts were an inferior brand, constructed of cheap fabric and worn at the cuffs. "They weren't shirts a man like the one I met with Caroline would wear."

"So there could be another man," Rachel said.

A man at the opposite end of the financial spectrum. "There is the possibility that Preston Wellington III found out about the other man," Samantha told her boss.

"Which you think could mean Caroline's hit-and run was no accident," Rachel said.

"It does make me wonder since Alex Graham and I seemed to have picked up a tail. I can't help but wonder what someone is afraid we're going to find out."

VICTOR CONSTANTINE was used to taking orders. He wasn't even that particular who was doing the ordering but he had to admit, he didn't like his latest job any more than he liked the arrogant voice on the other end of the line.

He had two simple rules. He never knew who he was working for. He didn't care. And his jobs came in by word of mouth, which meant he only did jobs for clients who'd been referred through other clients. The kind of people who had the kind of money required for his unique services.

It made his life easier that way. He received a call, waited for the money to appear electronically in a numbered account and then he did the job.

The more dangerous the job, the more money went into his account. Victor had an ironclad reputation for getting the job done, no matter how dirty. It had made him a rich man, a man on the verge of retiring at a very young age.

That's why he was having trouble taking orders from his latest "client." The guy was an arrogant bastard, Victor thought as he dialed the number he'd been given.

The man didn't even say hello. "Where the hell are you? I told you to let me know what was going on."

Victor was hot, tired and hungry and he didn't like being talked to like this. "Why do you think I'm calling?" he snapped, silently reminding himself how much he was getting paid. His fees tended to triple when he didn't like the job—or the client.

Victor glanced up the street. "After the hospital, he drove to Weddings Your Way, picked up a woman and drove to a seedy part of town." He gave the client the address and heard the man let out an oath under his breath.

"The woman is still with him?"

Victor described her. "They're in some dive of a Mexican café across the street eating dinner."

"He took her out to *eat?*"

Yeah, exactly what Victor should have been doing right now instead of sitting down the street in the dark. "Apparently so. I'd like to have some dinner myself."

"I don't pay you to eat."

"You don't pay me enough to miss meals, either."

Silence. "I'm sorry you missed your supper. But with what I pay you, I'm sure you can order in later."

Victor smiled to himself. The man had no idea.

"Call me when they leave the restaurant and stay with them. Don't let them out of your sight." The line went dead.

Victor stared down at the phone for a moment, then thought, what the hell. He called information, got the number of the Mexican café and ordered himself the nightly special: a plate of seafood enchiladas, beans and rice.

"Do you want that delivered?" the female voice on the other end of the line inquired.

Victor smiled. "As a matter of fact I'm parked just down the street. There is a big tip in it if you get it out to me in a hurry."

As SAMANTHA returned to the café, she glanced at the other tables. A few people had come in. But none were singles. None, she surmised, was the person who'd been following them.

Alex looked up as if sensing her return, never taking his eyes off her from the time she started toward the table until she sat down.

It didn't just surprise her that he could unnerve her the way he did. It scared her. The wall she'd thrown up and her cool reserve, coupled with the way she dressed and acted, kept most men at a distance. But then Alex Graham wasn't most men. That point was starting to hit home.

"Thank you," he said when she was seated again. "You've been great tonight. I can't tell you how much I appreciate you going with me to the condo. I really don't think I could have done that alone. You've been amazing."

She felt embarrassed by the compliment. "I'm just glad I could help." *Help, indeed,* she thought with a stab of guilt at just the thought of returning to the condo for the champagne bottle and glasses. Who was helping whom?

"So tell me. How did you become a wedding planner?"

She picked up a corn chip and gave him her standard reply. "You wouldn't believe it if I told you."

"Try me."

She looked at him and saw that he seemed to genuinely be interested. Maybe too interested? Talking about that part of her job seemed safe enough. As if being here in this dark intimate café with Alex was safe.

"Well, there's not much to tell," she said, going with the abbreviated version. "I met Rachel and she offered me the job. I had no experience but I guess she saw what a detail person I am…."

"You had no experience as a wedding planner? You don't strike me as one of those women who always dreamed of her own wedding day," he said.

She'd been playing with the chip but now set it down on her napkin. She could feel the heat of his gaze and felt her throat go dry. "No. I always thought I'd elope." Her smile felt like plastic left out too long in the sun. "But I can understand why some couples want a large wedding. For most people it's the biggest event they will ever…" He'd made her remember how she'd once pictured her own wedding.

"Endure?" he suggested when she didn't go on.

She could only nod.

"Frankly? It sounds awful," he said as if he'd seen her discomfort. "Months of planning and hassle for a few minutes before a preacher. Months and months of planning."

She took a drink of the beer the waiter put in front

of her, thankful to him for saving her from a strained silence. "It *does* take a lot of planning because basically you're putting on a theatrical production not that much different from a Broadway play."

"Interesting perspective and appropriate since a wedding has so little to do with a marriage, don't you think?"

She smiled. "The wedding is fantasy, that's for sure. Some more than others. Look at some of the popular wedding themes. Antony and Cleopatra, Romeo and Juliet, Lancelot and Guinevere and then there are Royalty and Fairyland weddings, weddings In the Clouds, On the Rooftop, By the Sea…"

He laughed. "I had no idea." He shook his head, seeming to be enjoying himself. "No wonder I've never gotten married." He turned serious. "I don't mean to make light of what you do, but it really is a lot of smoke and mirrors, isn't it."

If he only knew. Both of her jobs were a lot of both. She began to relax. "We joke that we're in show business. But if you put on a great show everyone is happy and that's what it's all about."

They snacked on the chips and salsa for a few moments, a comfortable silence falling between them.

"Three months isn't enough for the type of show my father wants, is it," he said after a while.

"Not really," she admitted. "I'm going to have to pull a few rabbits out of my hat but don't worry, I won't let your sister down."

He smiled almost ruefully. "I'm sure you won't but it might not be a problem. There might not be a wedding because there might not be a groom." He held up his hands as if in surrender. "I know. You're convinced this fiancé of hers is in love with her and wouldn't desert her—especially pregnant. I hope you're right."

So did she, but it was getting tougher to keep making excuses for Preston Wellington III.

ALEX COULDN'T REMEMBER a meal he'd enjoyed more. While Caroline was never far from his thoughts, he stopped obsessing over her missing fiancé. He liked the idea of being an uncle. It wasn't like Caroline would be alone or penniless. He would see to that.

Even though he wasn't sure he should, he liked Samantha Peters. She'd drawn him out, asking about his job as a fireman. She'd seemed genuinely interested and had laughed at his stories from the firehouse. He'd steered clear of the anguish that often came with his job.

As they finished their meal, he asked, "The woman who was abducted. Have they found her?"

Samantha shook her head. "There's been no word."

He was shocked to hear it and even more shocked to realize he hadn't given the other woman a thought. He'd been too involved with his sister's hit-and-run.

"I'm sorry," he said. "You think she was kidnapped?"

"I don't know."

"But no ransom demand has been made yet?" he

asked, still convinced that there had to be a connection between his sister and the driver of that car.

"Not that I've heard."

"Thank you again," he said. Just looking at her made him feel better.

"It's been my pleasure—" She broke off, seemingly a little flustered. It wasn't like her and he found himself smiling at her again. "I enjoyed dinner," she amended.

"Me, too." His gaze locked with hers, her brown eyes seeming to shimmer. He wanted to reach across the table and remove her glasses, brush her hair back from her face and—

Her cell phone rang. He watched her glance at the caller ID and saw her expression change.

"I'm sorry," she said. "I need to take this."

He nodded, the moment lost as she got up and stepped away from the table. He didn't know if he should feel disappointment. Or relief. He had been about to make a fool of himself.

"PETERS," SAMANTHA SAID into the phone, hoping this was going to be good news.

"Samantha, it's Rachel. I just wanted to let you know that you were right about the black limo. Looks like it was stolen off a car lot in Fort Lauderdale. Matches the description."

"Has the car been found?" Samantha asked, glad she had gotten something right since there was a good chance that she'd been wrong about Caroline's fiancé.

"Not yet," Rachel said. "How are things at your end?"

Interesting. "Fine," she said glancing back toward the table and Alex. "I'm still going by the hospital tonight. I thought I'd drop in on Craig Johnson. I know it's late, but maybe he's remembered something. I'll visit Caroline tomorrow, instead."

"Good idea."

She rang off and walked back to the table.

Alex was just putting his cell phone away. He'd paid their dinner bill and looked anxious.

"I should get to the hospital. Would you mind if we stopped on the way back?" he asked, rising.

She'd hoped to go to the hospital alone but maybe she could make this work and save herself a trip since she would have to go back to the condo as it was. "Of course not. Is everything all right?"

He nodded, his expression grim. "No change."

Samantha felt the weight of his disappointment and her own. She'd been on such a roller coaster of emotions. Now, she felt too warm from the spicy food and the entertaining company. Mostly, she'd felt too content just before the phone call from Rachel.

And that was dangerous. She needed to get back to work behind the scenes, back to what made her feel safe and that was far away from Alex Graham.

At the hospital, they rode together up the elevator to Caroline's floor. "I'll wait here for you," she said as he started down the hall. She noticed that a guard had been posted outside Caroline's door. "Is that your doing?" she asked, surprised.

"I hired guards 24-7 to keep an eye on her. I'm still not convinced the hit-and-run was an accident. And until I am…"

"Can't hurt having the guard here, especially if it makes you feel better."

"*You* make me feel better," he said touching her hand and seeming not to notice when she flinched at his surprise touch. "I won't be long."

"Take your time. Really."

She headed down the hall toward the nurses' station, slowing as Alex nodded to the private guard and entered his sister's room. Before the door closed, Samantha caught a glimpse of Caroline lying in the bed surrounded by equipment. It was so sad to see this beautiful, young woman bandaged and broken, let alone to think about the baby she was carrying.

In her line of work, Samantha dealt with bad guys all the time—just not up close and personal. For the first time, she was on the front lines and she'd never wanted to see justice done more than she did right now. She would do anything to find the person behind Sonya Botero's abduction, behind Caroline Graham's hit-and-run—even if it turned out that she'd been wrong about Preston Wellington III and he was involved.

She walked down to the nurses' station on the pretense of inquiring about Caroline Graham's condition. As she spoke with the nurse, Samantha noted Craig

Johnson's room number. It was just up the hall from Caroline's room.

Alex was still in with his sister as Samantha passed the guard. She waited until he was busy reading a magazine in his chair outside Caroline's door before Samantha headed for the chauffeur-bodyguard's room.

She recalled what she'd witnessed earlier from the front window of Weddings Your Way. The driver of the car carrying the men who'd abducted Sonya Botero had appeared to purposely try to run down Johnson before striking Caroline Graham. Had there been more than one target?

She hesitated at the door to Johnson's room. According to the Miami Confidential team, he was complaining of headaches and claiming he couldn't recall anything about the incident.

Talking to him would no doubt prove to be a waste of time and possibly make Johnson suspicious, but maybe he had remembered something by now. Something that would help.

She pushed the door to his room partially open and stopped at the sound of his raised voice. He was speaking to someone, his tone strained.

She froze as he moved into her field of vision and she saw that he was on the phone, pacing back and forth in front of the window, his back to her. Cautiously he lifted a corner of the blind and peered out to the street.

"I'm telling you they tried to run me down," Johnson said. "I was almost killed. What if they try again?"

So much for him not remembering anything about the incident, she thought, and wondered if he might be right about being in danger. But why kill him? There were other witnesses at the scene.

Thinking of the killers hitting Johnson here at the hospital, she heard movement behind her and whirled around, all her FBI self-defense training coming back in a rush.

ALEX HARDLY RECOGNIZED the woman who spun on him, her hands going up in a self-defense move. He jerked back in nothing short of shock. Even Samantha's expression wasn't one he'd seen before. She looked ready to kick his butt. More than that, she looked scared as if she'd been expecting someone to harm her.

"You all right?" he asked, glancing toward the hospital door she'd just let close. He'd caught her eavesdropping. Had she overheard something that frightened her?

"Sorry," she said instantly, seeming embarrassed. "You startled me."

"I guess."

"I was just checking to see how Mr. Johnson was doing."

Mr. Johnson, from what Alex had overheard, was the driver of the limo, the man who was attacked and his client abducted.

"He seems to be on the phone," Samantha said, with a nonchalance that she didn't quite pull off.

Alex had noticed Johnson on the phone when he'd come up behind her.

"How is Caroline?" Apparently she'd expected him to spend more time with his sister.

"The same," he said, wondering again about Samantha. Just about the time he thought he might be figuring her out, she threw him another curve.

Suddenly, he felt exhausted as if the day's events had finally caught up with him. "I should get you back," he said. "It's late. I didn't mean to take up so much of your time."

"Really, it hasn't been a problem. Dinner was wonderful, but I'll take a cab back," she said quickly as if she wanted to get away from him. "After the day you've had, you must be anxious to get home. Like you said, it's late, and you look drained. No reason to go out of your way."

How did she know that her office wasn't on his way home? "It's too late for you to go back to your office tonight anyway," he said, suddenly wondering where she lived and why she was trying to get rid of him. "Let me take you home. I'd be happy to give you a ride to work in the morning. Just tell me what time to be there."

She started to argue but he stopped her.

"I won't hear of you taking a cab. Not after you were kind enough to spend the evening with me. I really didn't want to be alone. So you must let me take you home."

"I have to go back to the office tonight before I can go home."

Why wasn't he surprised? "Well, then I'm taking you."

She nodded as if she'd accepted that he wasn't going to take no for an answer. But he could see that she would have much preferred taking a cab. Why was that? Earlier they'd been so close. But now she seemed uncomfortable in his presence and had been ever since he'd caught her listening in at the chauffeur's hospital room door. Or was it after he'd caught her in her self-defense mode and seen her expression?

Either way, he'd heard enough to know that this Mr. Johnson was scared—and that the man thought the driver of the black limo had purposely tried to kill him and might try again.

And all this just when Alex had almost convinced himself there was nothing going on, that Caroline's accident had been just that—an accident.

As they reached the outer door, he took Samantha's elbow and felt her jump at his touch—her reaction even more pronounced than it had been the other time.

Who was Samantha Peters—a woman who seemed to do everything possible not to be noticed?

Whatever her motivation, he told himself he had every right—and possibly every reason—to find out more about this woman his sister had been working with over the past six months.

Chapter Five

Victor Constantine had the worst case of heartburn he'd ever had in his life. He knew better than to eat spicy food. He parked down the street and watched as the woman got out of the man's pickup.

She had great legs, he noticed as she bent back into the truck to say something. Nice posterior, too. But that suit she wore was all wrong for her. The woman didn't have a clue how to accentuate her assets.

Victor had taken some classes the one and only time he was in the joint. He thought he would have made a pretty good designer. He had the eye. Maybe he would try to get back into that when he retired—which wouldn't be long and he would still be plenty young enough to make something of himself as a designer.

The chick shut the door and headed for the building again with the sign out front that read: Weddings Your Way.

Was she a wedding planner? That was interesting.

He sighed wishing he could call it a night as he un-snapped his cell phone and hit redial. "He just dropped the woman off at Weddings Your Way. You want me to follow him? Or her?"

"Her. Find out where she lives. While you're there, see what kind of security system she has at her house. Check the place out. You might be going in." Click.

Victor wasn't happy about breaking into the woman's house at some time in the future. While it meant he could charge the client even more, it also meant that this job wasn't going to be over as quickly as he'd hoped. His heartburn was killing him and now he would have to sit and wait.

He watched the man walk her to the door. Quite the gentleman. But what was she doing going back to an office this time of the night?

Rubbing his chest, Victor glanced down the street hoping to see a place he could buy some antacids, but the area was too hoity-toity to have a gas station or a convenience store. To add insult to injury, the car smelled like refried beans.

He thought again about bagging this job. The only thing that stopped him was the money. He had a pretty good idea where all this was headed given what a bastard he was working for. The end pay would be primo. It would be his last job. End on a good note.

Maybe he would become a designer. Or hell, a wedding planner. He would be great at either.

As Samantha closed the front door of Weddings Your Way behind her, she waited until Alex drove away before she headed straight upstairs to the secret room on the second floor.

"I had a feeling you'd still be here working," she said as she stepped in and closed the sealed door behind her.

Clare Myers turned from her computer. "You and I should really get lives, you know that," she said, grinning.

Samantha smiled as she pulled out a chair next to Clare. The only way to eliminate Caroline Graham's fiancé as a suspect was to find him and she hoped Clare would be able to help. "I need to find out everything I can about Preston Wellington III."

"You still haven't been able to contact him?" Clare asked, sounding surprised.

"No. And I'm starting to worry." She gave Clare all the information she had on the missing fiancé—which she realized wasn't much.

"How is Caroline Graham doing?"

"She might not make it and she's pregnant."

"Oh, no," Clare said. "I'll see what I can do to find him for you. I planned to do a preliminary search earlier but I got sidetracked doing some checking on the Sonya Botero and Juan DeLeon side of the investigation."

"Still nothing on that end?"

Clare shook her head. "They say in the case of a kidnapping that the first twenty-four hours are critical."

That explained what Clare was still doing here.

Clare's words stuck in her mind as Samantha headed

down the stairs toward her office. She hoped to have something on her end of the case by then, as well. Unfortunately, she was starting to wonder if Alex's concerns might be justified.

As she reached the ground floor, she heard the phone in her office ringing.

She thought about letting the machine pick it up. If it was Rachel, she would use Samantha's cell. Other than Clare, no one knew she was here and from the ring she could tell it wasn't an inside-the-office line.

Surely whoever was calling wouldn't expect her to be in her office. Not at this hour.

Unless it was Alex.

Maybe he'd thought of something he'd forgotten to tell her. Because he was the only one who knew she was here.

Or was he?

She thought about the tail and with a chill, picked up the phone, automatically touching her keypad to be sure the shop's security system was up and working tonight. She hadn't noticed the tail after they'd left the hospital but that didn't mean anything. She'd been distracted after being caught outside Craig Johnson's room.

"Hello?" she said into the phone.

At first she heard nothing, then the sound of breathing. Great, an obscene phone call. Just to prove this day couldn't get any worse.

She started to hang up when an obviously disguised voice said, "You're making a mistake. Stop butting into

Caroline Graham's life or you'll regret it." There was a click. The caller was gone.

A chill wound around her neck like a garrote.

Samantha hit star 69 but the number was blocked. The phone rang and rang. No answer.

She hung up, confused and even more afraid for Caroline. Samantha would have sworn that Sonya Botero's abduction had nothing to do with Caroline Graham. Maybe it still didn't. But something was definitely going on with Caroline. Beginning—and possibly ending—with her missing fiancé.

One thing kept bothering Samantha. The men's clothing in Caroline Graham's closet. They hadn't just been old. They'd been cheap. Not the kind of shirts a rich man wore even when he was doing manual labor.

But the Preston Wellington III that Samantha had met at Weddings Your Way dressed like a rich man, acted like a rich man, to all appearances *was* a rich man on the same financial playing field as Caroline Graham. He wouldn't be doing manual labor. He would hire it done.

So that left the big question: Whose shirts were those in Caroline's closet?

Someone had followed them after they'd left the condo. She had to assume the caller knew she'd been to the condo tonight. Knew she and Alex were digging into Caroline's life—and Preston Wellington III's.

That meant there must be something to find.

More and more Samantha thought Alex had been smart to put a private guard outside his sister's hospital room. Caroline might be in serious danger. And Preston Wellington III could be the person she had to fear most.

SAMANTHA HAD NO CHOICE—especially after that threatening phone call.

She would have to go back to Caroline's condo tonight and get the champagne bottle and glasses. It was time to find out what was going on.

She considered who the caller might have been. The list of suspects was fairly short at this point. It came down to who had something to hide.

Right now that seemed to be Preston Wellington III since no one had heard from him.

Samantha didn't even want to think what that meant. She'd liked the man. What did that say for her instincts? Nothing good.

One way or the other, she had to answer some nagging questions about him and what had happened to Caroline. There'd been no word on Sonya Botero and the clock was ticking.

But first Samantha had to make sure she wasn't followed this time. She checked her gun. Fully loaded with an extra clip in the bottom of her bag.

She added two large evidence bags and a pair of latex gloves to her oversize shoulder bag, then leaving the light on in her office, she went into her private restroom and changed her clothing, stripping out of the business suit and dressing in black running gear.

She pulled her hair up and under a black hat and

checked herself in the mirror, pleased. Then she left by the back way.

The humid Florida air hit her as she stepped from the air-conditioned building into the well-lit staff parking area under Weddings Your Way. Sliding into her small black sports car convertible, she turned the key.

The car was the only hint of the woman Samantha kept hidden from most people. The one crack in her armor. Her one little secret vice since she drove a midsize white sedan except on those rare occasions that called for cloak-and-dagger, speed or letting the real her out under the cover of darkness.

The engine roared to life with a throaty rumble that made her smile. *Catch me if you can.*

She blasted out of the parking garage and onto the street. A set of headlights flashed on behind her. She could imagine the driver half asleep, bored, caught off guard since her office light was still on. And in this car, he couldn't be sure he was even following the right person.

Samantha smiled to herself and gunned the engine, rocketing around a corner, then another. Losing her tail had been almost too easy. But she still zigzagged her way to Caroline's condo enjoying the feel of the night air.

"WHAT THE HELL do you mean *you lost her?*"

Victor swallowed back the bile rising in his throat. After he'd lost her, he'd stopped at a drugstore and bought himself some antacids but they were taking their sweet time working.

"I can't even be sure it was her," he said, hating the apologetic tone of his voice. He was a professional. How had he let a snip of a wedding planner trick him like that? The light was still on in her office when the little black sports car had come flying out of the back of the place. "She switched cars on me." She'd had a head start and was driving like a bat out of hell. Driving nothing like he had expected her to do.

"So maybe she's still at her office?"

He swore under his breath. "I don't think so. I think that was her. Given the way she dresses, it was unlikely but still…"

A curse on the other end of the line. "Never mind. I'll take care of it. Go home. I'll call you when I need you." The line went dead.

The antacids were starting to work. Victor Constantine began to breathe a little easier.

But he didn't go home. Instead, he circled back to Weddings Your Way. He had a hunch. And he wasn't going to be able to sleep until his heartburn got better anyway. She'd fooled him once. But she wouldn't again.

THE SAME GUARD was on duty as when Samantha had been to the renewal project with Alex. She spotted him from a safe distance but avoided detection by parking some distance away and keeping to the darkness as she worked her way to Caroline's condo.

There were no lights on in any of the buildings. Apparently it was true that Caroline's was the only one occupied.

to the bedroom door. She knew only too well where those kinds of thoughts would get her.

She had just started to open the door when she heard a warning sound on the other side. Before she could react, though, the door flew open, slamming into her and driving her back. As she fell next to the bed, her shoulder bag smacking the floor next to her, she heard one of the expensive glasses shatter.

She groped for her bag—and her gun—as a dark figure filled the bedroom doorway. She couldn't see his face. In the dim light coming in from the street through the plastic behind him, he was nothing more than a blurred silhouette.

But from his stance, she could tell he held a gun in one hand and he was trying to find her in the dark bedroom, no doubt afraid to turn on the light for fear that she would see him—and possibly get off the first shot.

Her hand found her bag. Carefully, she slid her hand in until her fingers closed on the gun's grip.

ALEX GRAHAM couldn't sleep. In the kitchen, he took a beer from the fridge and wandered through the house, feeling lost and unsettled.

He had way too much on his mind. Caroline. Preston Wellington III. Samantha Peters.

He remembered her face in the warm lights of the café, the soft cadence of her voice, her engaging smile. He found himself smiling at just the thought of her.

His smile faded at the memory of her expression

when she'd turned away from the chauffeur's hospital room door. She'd been on the offense, ready to strike out, expecting someone else behind her.

Why would a wedding planner instantly think she had to defend herself? Especially in a hospital with a guard right down the hall?

And it didn't seem like her style, eavesdropping like that. Nor had she been happy when he'd caught her at it.

He frowned and realized how little he'd learned about her after spending hours with her this evening. When he thought about it, he recalled how she'd side-stepped any personal questions, turning the conversation back to ask about him.

Maybe it was just part of her training as a wedding planner. Like self-defense?

He shook his head. Nothing odd about a single woman knowing self-defense. That wasn't what was bothering him. He couldn't put his finger on it but at every turn he felt there was a hell of a lot more going on with Samantha Peters than she wanted him to know. Than maybe she wanted *anyone* to know.

He took a sip of his beer and spied his sister's purse lying on the table by the door where he'd dropped it earlier. The hospital had insisted he take it home with him.

He'd only made a cursory search of the purse looking for keys, Preston's phone number, his sister's home address.

Now he wished he hadn't seen where she'd been staying. All it had done was leave him more upset and worried. What was going on with her? When he'd called his father, he hadn't mentioned what he'd found out. But when he'd asked about where Caroline was living, his father had said she was staying with a friend while some new place of hers was being renovated. Basically it didn't sound like C.B. knew any more than Alex did.

And where was Preston Wellington III?

Not knowing anything was driving him crazy.

He retrieved his sister's purse and took it to the couch where he sat down, and after a moment's hesitation, dumped the contents out on the coffee table.

He had no idea what he was looking for as he rummaged through the assortment of makeup and vitamins and lotions in between taking drinks of his beer. The bag was like a small drugstore. Did his beautiful sister really need all this beauty stuff?

He picked up her wallet, opened it and found a dozen different credit cards, her driver's license, a few snapshots. One of a good-looking man who he assumed was Preston. Another of Alex himself. It was an outdated family photograph when he and Caroline and Brian were kids.

Guilt stabbed through him. He'd made no effort to get along with his family for years. Hell, he'd had a chip on his shoulder as big as a California redwood.

Maybe that's why Caroline had called him today and wanted him to meet her at the wedding planner's. Because she was hoping to bring the family back together before her wedding. Maybe that's all there had been to it. And her hit-and-run had been just an accident.

He had to admit he liked the idea of being close to his sister again. No chance of him being close to his brother, Brian. Or even their father. He was barely civil with them and he didn't feel as though it was all his fault. But he could try for Caroline's sake, he promised himself. He would do anything—if she would just get better.

He opened her checkbook and was surprised to see how low her balance was.

And then he saw why. He would have expected her most recent checks to be to Miami's most expensive clothing stores. Instead they were for plumbing and lighting fixtures, drywall contractors and material, lumber.

He sat up, spilling his beer. What the hell? She was footing the bill for all the renovations to the condo? Where was this fiancé of hers? And why wasn't he paying for the repairs?

Then Alex saw something that stopped his heart cold. Check after check to the same company: Wellington Enterprises, a company no doubt owned by his sister's missing fiancé.

SAMANTHA COULD TELL that the man in the doorway hadn't seen where she'd fallen. He was listening, trying to find her in the dark room.

She told herself he might be the security guard. But she hoped a security guard would have more sense than to silhouette himself in a doorway. And the security guard would have said something by now.

Whoever this man was, she could hear him breathing hard. He was either scared or winded. Or both. He was swinging the gun back and forth in a short arc, his hands shaking, indicating he had little experience with a firearm. But even an inexperienced gunman could kill her at this close range.

It was a chance she wasn't willing to take.

She didn't dare move. Nor take a breath. She knew she didn't have time to draw her gun from her bag before he would hear the sound and fire. Her only hope was to draw his attention to another part of the room.

She inched her hand free under the bed, remembering the clothing that had been tossed across the end of it. She was betting on what she would find and was rewarded when her fingers closed around a high-heeled shoe, just as she'd suspected.

Moving in slow motion, she drew it from under the bed, careful not to make a sound. She couldn't hold her breath much longer. With luck, he wouldn't see her movements—just hear the shoe drop.

She had to be ready. Once she threw the shoe she would have to move quickly.

She needed to breathe, to move from her awkward position on the floor. She counted to three and launched the high heel through the open bathroom doorway.

The gunman swung in that direction and fired off two quick shots, the sound of breaking glass raining down on the tile floor. The huge mirror over the sink had shattered, making more noise than the shots especially since the gun he carried seemed to have a silencer on it.

Under the cover of the racket, Samantha scrambled up, staying in a low crouch and swung her gun toward the door.

She'd been trained to kill when necessary. Not that she'd ever had to kill anyone. She didn't want tonight to be the first. Especially if the man with the gun was Caroline Graham's fiancé.

But the doorway was empty.

She blinked. He couldn't have had time to come into the room. He must have stepped to a side of the door. That meant he was waiting for her to make her next move.

Listening, she waited, afraid he had somehow slipped into the room. That he might even be hiding in the closet. Or on the other side of the bed.

Then she heard the rattle of plastic.

He was making a run for it!

She rushed to the doorway, dodged to one side, and took a quick look around the edge of the doorjamb in case it was a trick.

She heard the thunder of footfalls and took off after him. As she pushed through the plastic and turned the corner toward the door, something solid struck her in the face just below her left eye and dropped her to her knees.

She blinked back stars and blackness as she grabbed the wall to keep from passing out. She could hear the sound of heavy footfalls, the sound of him retreating down the stairs, getting away.

She tried to get to her feet, but the blackness closed in and she had to sit down in the Sheetrock dust and lean her head back against the wall.

It wasn't until she turned on her penlight that she saw what he'd thrown at her. A foot-long piece of two-by-four lumber.

No chance of any prints on the board. She waited until the dizziness and darkness stopped, then she returned to the bedroom to retrieve her shoulder bag.

VICTOR CONSTANTINE felt a hundred times better. The antacids had done their job. He'd opened the car window while waiting down the street from Weddings Your Way and the refried beans smell was almost gone.

But that wasn't why he felt so good.

He'd had a hunch that the wedding planner would return to her office. And she had.

He'd been taken off guard when she'd switched cars the first time. But now she returned, with the top down on the sleek black sports car convertible, her hat gone and her hair blowing in the wind. He wondered where she'd been and what she'd been up to.

He'd waited, figuring she would switch cars again. And she had, driving a white sedan—just as he'd been told she drove.

Following her at a safe distance now, he couldn't help but wonder why he'd been hired to follow her and the man he knew only as Alex, although he'd found out that Alex drove a pickup, worked as a fireman and that his last name was Graham. He'd never wondered about why he was hired by his clients. It was dangerous.

But this time, he found himself considering what his

client was so afraid these two were going to find out. A fireman and a wedding planner. Hell, how dangerous could they be?

Several things about the two did make him wonder. One, the car switching and how fast the wedding planner drove. And that she went home alone. What was wrong with this Alex guy that he'd let that happen?

Victor looked up and realized he didn't see her car. He sped up. No way had she seen him tailing her. No way. Traffic was light. If she could have turned, he would have seen her. But somehow she'd given him the slip. Again.

She must have suspected someone might follow her.

But how had she known how to lose him like that?

Who the hell was this woman?

Victor Constantine planned to find out.

SAMANTHA THOUGHT she would never be able to get to sleep. Her mind raced with the day's events, her thoughts always circling back to Alex Graham.

She took a hot bath and climbed naked between the cool sheets, her head aching from where she'd been struck by the board at the condo. Her body also aching for a man's touch. Not any man's touch. Alex Graham's. She squeezed her eyes shut, praying for sleep. Praying for Sonya and Caroline.

The next thing she knew she was awakened by the phone. "Hello?"

For some reason she thought it would be Alex.

Probably because he'd been on her mind again right before she'd fallen asleep.

"I woke you. Sorry," Clare said. "But I knew you'd want this right away."

Samantha sat up. Clare couldn't have already heard from the lab with a match on the fingerprints from the champagne bottle or glasses. It hadn't been that long ago that Samantha had dropped them off.

She turned on the lamp and glanced at the clock beside her bed. "What are you doing still working at this hour of the night?"

"Couldn't sleep."

Samantha knew that feeling. Normally.

"It's about Preston Wellington III."

She felt her heart leap in her throat. Something had happened to him. Isn't that what she'd been afraid of?

"According to every record available in the U.S., no one by that name exists," Clare said.

"*What?*" She sat up straighter, trying to make sense of what Clare was saying.

"No record of a birth, social security card, employment, library card, school attendance, graduation, marriage or death. Nada," Clare said. "There was no Preston Wellington III. Until a year ago."

Samantha groaned. "You're sure?"

Clare chuckled. "He must have made some impression."

"It wasn't just him. They were one of the few couples who made me think, 'Wow, they truly love each other.

These two might really make it.' He seemed so head-over-heels for her. How could I be so wrong?"

"She's rich? And he's one hell of an actor?" Clare suggested. "You know what amazes me? That someone with Caroline Graham's money wouldn't be suspicious of every man she met. I'd run a check on the man before I even dated him—let alone agreed to marry him. I guess the old adage is true: Love is blind."

"She must not have wanted to know," Samantha said, thinking about the shirts in the closet at the condo. Love was indeed blind—and stupid, she thought. "Well, if Preston Wellington III is just some name he's taken, then who is he?"

"Your guess is as good as mine. I see your note here about sending some fingerprints to be analyzed? If his prints are on file, I guess we'll know soon enough."

If his prints were on file. Samantha had a bad feeling they would be and not because of some employment requirement. She wouldn't be surprised now to learn that the man had a record. After all, Caroline's fiancé had already proven himself a liar. Chances were good he would have had a run-in with the law.

In fact, chances were even better that Samantha had run into him tonight at the condo.

Chapter Six

The next morning on her way into Weddings Your Way, Samantha passed Juan DeLeon leaving. Sonya Botero's fiancé was tall, dark and incredibly good-looking but today he appeared shattered, like a man who feared he'd lost everything. The expression on his handsome face broke her heart.

To find someone you wanted to spend the rest of your life with and to lose them— The thought broke off abruptly as she recalled the single time she'd felt that way. And how incredibly wrong she had been.

It wasn't long after that that Rachel had approached her about working with the Miami Confidential team. She'd been ecstatic. Until she heard what their cover was.

"Weddings?"

"Is that a problem?" Rachel had asked her, sounding surprised by her reaction.

"No," Samantha had quickly covered, cursing silently to herself. *Weddings?*

It was hard sometimes seeing how happy the brides were. Like Caroline Graham.

And Sonya Botero.

It had been almost twenty-four hours and still there was no ransom demand, no word at all. Where was Sonya? Who had taken her?

Samantha was reminded of last night and the man who'd tried to kill her in Caroline's condo. She quickly went to her ultra neat desk and pulled out her appointment book.

If Preston Wellington III had been after Caroline Graham's money and that plan was soured by her pregnancy, maybe he saw a way to still get the fortune he was after.

She leafed through her appointment book, already knowing what she was going to find. Sonya Botero's appointment had been right after Caroline Graham's.

That meant that Caroline's fiancé would have seen Sonya. Had he found out who she was? More to the point, had he found out *what* she was worth?

Samantha shuddered at the thought, shocked by what that could mean. Was it possible that Sonya Botero's alleged kidnapping was nothing more than a smoke screen for the true crime—the murder of Caroline Graham.

Samantha went into the small kitchen adjacent to her office and made herself a cup of tea, feeling chilled and needing the calm that hot tea always brought her. Taking the cup to her office window, she looked out over Biscayne Bay. The water shimmered in the sunlight.

Several sailboats leaned in the breeze, canvases bright white against the blue horizon.

"Samantha?"

She turned to find Rachel standing in the doorway of her office.

"I was waiting for your report," her boss said.

"I was just going to check in," Samantha said quickly.

Rachel closed the door and moved deeper into the office, stopping short when she saw the cut and dark bruise that even makeup couldn't hide on Samantha's cheek.

Without further hesitation, Rachel slid into a chair, motioning for Samantha to do the same. "What happened?"

Samantha touched the injury and winced. "Some of my skills in the field are a little rusty, but I got what I went for." She told Rachel what had happened. "I'm just waiting to hear from the lab."

Fortunately the champagne glass that had broken when she'd fallen was the one with the lipstick on it and the pieces were large enough that the lab would probably still be able to lift a print or two from it.

"Caroline Graham hasn't regained consciousness?" Rachel asked.

Samantha shook her head. "Luckily, the baby is all right. At least so far."

"And the fiancé?"

She shrugged. "He's still missing. And on top of that he's not Preston Wellington III. No person by that name existed until a year ago—about the time Caroline met him."

Rachel looked surprised. "I saw him come in with Caroline. I didn't suspect a thing."

"Neither did I. I really believed he was in love with her. That they were in love with each other. And this morning, I did some checking. Caroline and Sonya had some appointments after each other. Preston or whoever he is would have seen Sonya, might even have learned who she was." She realized what she was saying. The man was looking even more like a suspect in Sonya Botero's abduction as well as Caroline's hit-and-run.

Rachel didn't look pleased to hear the news. "Did you talk to Craig Johnson last night at the hospital?"

She told Rachel about her visit to the hospital and what she'd overheard in Craig Johnson's hospital room. "He sounded scared. I have a feeling the reason he is complaining of a headache and memory loss is so he can stay in the hospital where he feels safer." She went on to tell her boss about the threatening phone call she'd received.

Rachel took in the information. "Do you think Caroline should have some protection on her at the hospital?"

"Alex hired a private guard to stay outside his sister's room just down the hall."

"Alex?" She gave Samantha a questioning look.

Samantha felt her face flush and realized the way she'd said his name had cued her boss. "He insists I call him by his first name."

"Of course he would." Rachel smiled, studying her. "I've never seen you flustered like this before, though. Are you sure you're all right?"

"It's Alex. Mr. Graham. He…" She shook her head. "He's rather intense and he doesn't miss much. I have to watch myself around him all the time."

Rachel frowned. "I've seen you turn hysterical bridezillas into purring pussycats, deal with drunk wedding guests and irate fiancés, but if you think you can't handle Alex Graham…"

"No, I can handle him," Samantha said with more confidence than she felt. She was a trained professional. Surely she could handle one handsome fireman. One very handsome, charming, intelligent fireman. "If I tried to hand him off to someone else on the team now, it would only make him more suspicious. He's suspicious enough that we're hiding something from him."

"Under the circumstances, I suppose we can't blame him," Rachel said.

"Any news on Sonya Botero?" Samantha asked, not wanting to discuss Alex Graham further.

"No. No ransom demand. Nothing."

"I saw Juan DeLeon as I was coming in," Samantha said. "He looked devastated."

"He is. He's inconsolable, blaming himself for Sonya's presumed kidnapping," Rachel said. "He assumes, as we do, that it's politically driven, but he hasn't been able to find out who's behind it and neither have we."

Samantha nodded. "I suppose the wedding will be postponed."

"No. He insists we continue with the wedding prep-arations vowing that there will be a wedding in August,"

Rachel said. "He refuses to believe he might have lost her. That's why you have to stay on this end of the investigation. If Caroline Graham's fiancé lied about who he was, who knows what else he might be hiding."

Samantha nodded absently and realized she'd been thinking about Alex again and hadn't heard what Rachel had just said. "Sorry?"

Rachel cleared her throat. "I was saying I want you to continue working on this end of the investigation. Clare hasn't been able to come up with any connection between Sonya and Caroline other than what you have about them possibly crossing paths here. But let's not take any chances especially given what we know about the fiancé. The fact that he's missing worries me."

Me, too, Samantha thought.

"The rest of the team will be working on the theory that Sonya's abduction is political and connected to the assassination attempt on Juan DeLeon and the unrest in his country." Rachel rose to leave. "Be careful," she said her gaze going again to Samantha's bruised cheek. "Keep your eye on Alex Graham. He could be more dangerous than you think."

Samantha already suspected just how dangerous Alex could be—at least to her. That's why he had her running scared.

"I'll write up my report and then make sure everything is ready for the Holcom-Anders wedding," Samantha said, mentally shifting gears back to her other job.

Rachel had stopped in the doorway. "Are you sure you don't want me to put someone else on this?"

Samantha wasn't completely sure if she meant the wedding, or Alex Graham. "I have it covered."

Rachel seemed to study her again as if trying to make up her mind about something.

"The next time Alex Graham sees me I hope to be working on the Holcom-Anders wedding," Samantha said. "I think the best thing that could happen is for him to see me doing my job as a wedding planner."

Rachel nodded. "Yes, I think you're right about that. Watch your back. In this business, you never know who you can trust." She could just as easily have been talking about the wedding planning business as their sideline.

But Samantha was more worried right now about when she would see Alex Graham again—and how to break the bad news about Preston Wellington III. Alex was no fool. He wasn't going to believe this kind of information just fell into a wedding planner's lap.

The last thing she wanted was to make him more suspicious of Weddings Your Way—or worse, of her.

"Keep me informed," Rachel said as she saw someone come in through the front door of Weddings Your Way.

Samantha nodded distractedly, knowing that Alex wasn't going to give up on finding Preston Wellington III, either.

"Sonya's father Carlos Botero," Rachel said quietly and straightened her immaculate suit as if bracing herself for the worst.

"What is going on?" Carlos Botero demanded as Rachel went to meet him.

Samantha couldn't hear the soft words that Rachel spoke to him as she led the older man to her office.

"I've already lost one daughter," Samantha heard Botero say. "I can't lose another." Rachel closed her office door.

NOT FAR AWAY, a man made a call he'd been dreading. "We haven't been able to get to DeLeon."

"You fool. First you botch his assassination attempt and now you mess up this, as well?"

"I got his woman."

A disapproving sound was made on the other end of the line. "You messed that up, as well, and you know it."

He ground his teeth. "DeLeon is too well guarded."

"Figure it out. But in the meantime, make sure you finish up the other job you were given. No mistakes this time. Clean up the mess you've made of this." The phone slammed down.

He sat for a moment, then clicked off his cell phone.

SAMANTHA SENSED Alex standing in her office doorway. Her gaze came up to meet his. For a moment neither spoke. She wouldn't have heard him over the hammer of her blood anyway.

He stepped in, closing the door behind him as he cleared his throat. "Sorry to bother you. I hate to ask but I was hoping you could help me with something. What happened?" he asked in alarm as he spotted her bruised, skinned cheek.

"Just clumsy," Samantha said. "I can't even remember what I bumped into."

She'd been expecting him but still her heart had started pounding when she'd looked up and seen him standing there. The man had that kind of effect on her. What had she been thinking telling Rachel she could handle this?

"Help you?" she managed to ask.

"I need to go see my father. I'd appreciate if you'd go with me. It might make it easier."

"I don't understand."

"You will when you meet my father. We don't get along." There was pain in his tone. "Truthfully? C.B. will be forced to be cordial with his daughter's wedding planner there. Otherwise, hell, it could turn into a knock-down-drag-out fight."

"I'm sure he isn't that bad," she said, smiling.

"Oh, I think you might be surprised." His smile lit up the office.

She looked down at the work on her desk just to give her a chance to regain her equilibrium. This was crazy. But this man of all men had awakened feelings in her she thought long buried. It was the last thing she needed. Or wanted. Especially under the circumstances.

"If you think your father will be more forthcoming with me there," she said, "then I'd be happy to help."

He chuckled at that, his gaze heating as he looked at

her. "My father has always had an appreciation for beautiful women."

She started to object since she was far from beautiful. She worked at being unexceptional. "You *must* be desperate. You're resorting to flattery."

"Just the truth," he said softly.

His eyes seemed deeper, richer and more vibrant tonight. But it was his gaze that started a slow simmer inside her. It had been so long since she'd felt anything. She fought the heat that shot through her veins and sent her pulse pounding in her ears. It scared her, feeling like this.

But at least Alex Graham had no clue as to who she really was. As long as he never got a glimpse of the woman she kept hidden, she was safe. She drew in a shaky breath and let it out slowly.

It was getting harder and harder to fight the feelings Alex Graham stirred in her. For that reason alone, she should have taken off running in the opposite direction.

ALEX WANTED TO believe Samantha's story about how she'd gotten the bruise on her cheek. Unfortunately, he just couldn't imagine her being clumsy. Nor could he shake the feeling that there was a lot more she wasn't telling him.

Not that it was any of his business.

He felt guilty. He'd coerced her into helping him. Dragging her first to Caroline's condo last night and now to the Graham lion's den. He knew what visits there were like. Hell. So why had he thought bringing her along would help?

Because there was something about her. Samantha tended to smooth troubled waters. She'd worked her magic on him and he'd seen the way she handled Caroline yesterday in her office.

But he knew his real reason. He still hadn't been able to shake the feeling that she knew more about what was going on than she was letting on. She'd at least spent time with Caroline—and Preston Wellington III—over the last six months. Maybe more time than anyone in his family.

He was also curious how she would fare with his father. C. B. Graham tended to overpower everyone he came in contact with. Would C.B. rattle Samantha? Alex was anxious to see. If he had to put his money on anyone it would be Samantha. She seemed impervious to the kind of browbeating his father was so good at. Hell, the woman had to deal with brides all day. Alex couldn't even imagine.

His father did like pretty young women. And as much as Samantha tried to hide her beauty, Alex didn't think his father would miss it any more than he had.

Alex pulled up to the gate and cursed under his breath as the attendant stepped out of his stone booth and gave Alex's pickup then Alex the once-over before hitting the button that opened the gate into the huge estate.

Samantha had said little on the drive and Alex hadn't

felt like trying to draw her out. He had too much on his mind. The last thing he wanted to do was to see his father.

"You grew up here?" Samantha asked now.

He glanced over at her. "You sound surprised."

"It's just that you seem so down-to-earth," she said, then seemed embarrassed as if she'd spoken without thinking, something he'd learned she seldom did.

He laughed. "I'm going to take that as a compliment."

He was sure in her business she'd seen her share of the rich and pretentious, but as he looked at the grounds and the huge mansion looming out of the palms, he saw it through her eyes.

"It takes ostentatious to a new level, don't you think?" he said. "I left here the first chance I got and haven't looked back."

"It's really magnificent."

"I suppose. I always felt like I couldn't breathe here. I guess it's the burden that comes with being a Graham. The price was too high."

He glanced over at her wondering about *her* background. It was impossible to explain to someone who didn't come from the kind of money the Graham family had what it was like. Most people thought if they had money their problems would be over.

After a winding lane of towering palms and flower-choked beds, Alex pulled around the circular drive and swore at the sight of his brother's sleek, red sports car parked out front.

"Great," he said, cutting the pickup's engine. "You're

going to get to meet my brother. Brian is always a real treat," he said sarcastically as he opened his door and hurried around to open hers.

She stepped out and he watched her take it all in, the massive white gleaming Spanish-style mansion, the English garden, the Olympic-size swimming pool and huge rock waterfalls, the six-car garage, the manmade lake, the guest cottages that were larger than most people's houses.

"I've only seen photographs of where the wedding was to be held," she said, sounding like a wedding planner again. "We hadn't gotten to the on-site preparations yet. I knew there was plenty of room but this is a phenomenal space for a wedding the size of your sister's."

How could the woman still think Caroline was getting married, let alone here. He couldn't imagine getting married here. If it didn't put a curse on the marriage he didn't know what would.

He took Samantha's elbow and walked her to the front door, smiling to himself as he felt her pulse jump at his touch.

SAMANTHA TRIED to find that cool calm she'd become famous for as she surreptitiously studied the man next to her. He rang the doorbell and waited. From inside the house came a few bars of a Mozart classic.

She felt jittery, even a little light-headed with her heart beating too quickly. She promised herself that when she returned to the office she would ask Rachel to put someone else on this case. She couldn't handle being around Alex Graham. Not for another second.

Alex fidgeted, clearly nervous and getting upset as he pressed the doorbell, holding it down this time. He'd been quiet driving here except for a brief thumbnail sketch of his family: father C.B., overbearing; Brian equally pretentious and overbearing and Caroline— That was where his expression softened. "Spoiled rotten." He'd smiled. "But you couldn't help but love her."

"Herbert," Alex said as the butler opened the door. Alex didn't wait for an invitation, just pushed past the uniformed stiff-necked man, drawing her with him as he ushered her into a foyer that was as big as the house she'd grown up in.

Herbert called after them, his voice echoing through the marbled entryway. "Was Mr. Graham expecting you?"

Alex gave a humorless laugh. "Not hardly," he said over his shoulder.

With Samantha in tow, he headed down the long tiled hallway. All she caught was a blur of crystal chandeliers and rich rare wood paneling.

At a large solid wood door, Alex stopped, took a breath and threw the door open exposing an opulent den and making the two men inside turn in surprise.

Both men wore suits, the younger man in an expensively cut navy pinstripe, the elder in a dark gray with a faint red thread running through the fabric. In this setting, they looked like a magazine ad for today's top executive and his dream office. The room around them was all glistening wood, supple dark leather and knee-deep carpet.

Their surprised gazes went from her to Alex and back again. Neither looked happy to see him.

She felt Alex stiffen next to her, his hand searching out hers. He squeezed it gently. "Welcome to the lion's den," he said under his breath, then stepped into the room, drawing her with him.

Chapter Seven

"Alex?" his father said, sounding as if he hadn't seen him in months and hardly recognized him. He hadn't.

Alex had gotten a glimpse of his father and Brian talking with Caroline's doctor at the hospital. He had hardly spoken to his father when he'd called yesterday to tell him about Caroline's accident.

Neither his father nor his brother had made an attempt to talk to him since and Alex hadn't bothered, either. He could only assume that his father blamed him for Caroline's accident. It would be just like C.B.

"Is this about Caroline? Is she—" His father's voice broke.

Alex shook his head. "She's still unconscious."

His father's look said, "Then why are you here?"

"I've been trying to contact her fiancé," Alex said. "Have you heard from him?"

C. B. Graham shook his head. "Pres spends quite a lot of time out of the country." Pres? "He's a busy man."

Yes, as C.B. had been when Alex was growing up.

What C.B. didn't say, but Alex heard: Unlike you, Alex, who only works part of the week as a fireman.

Alex felt that old frustration and resentment rising in him. Already his father had bonded with Preston Wellington III, practically a complete stranger, but C.B. made no effort to understand his youngest son.

Brian, Alex realized, was staring at Samantha.

"This is Samantha Peters. She's a wedding planner with Weddings Your Way. Caroline's been working with her."

"You're from the place where Caroline was struck down," Brian said with interest as if contemplating a lawsuit. He shifted his gaze to Alex. "What were you doing there with her anyway? I didn't even think the two of you had spoken in years."

"This must be very difficult for you all," Samantha broke in, stepping forward to shake each man's hand.

Alex watched in amazement as his father seemed to melt at her touch, at her softly spoken soothing words. What was it about this woman?

Brian, though, was his usual cold self. He seemed suspicious and angry. Nothing new there.

"Of course you're worried about Caroline, but she's in good hands," Samantha was saying. "All we can do now is find her fiancé. I know how devoted he is to her and he'd want to be here with her now."

C.B was practically falling all over himself saying,

"Yes, of course. He's a fine young man. This is such a tragedy with the wedding not that far off."

Did either his father or brother know that Caroline had moved the wedding up three months? Did they know she was pregnant?

"We've tried several numbers in an attempt to reach Mr. Wellington," Samantha was saying. "Any information you can give us would be appreciated."

"What exactly is your involvement, Miss…Peters was it?" Brian asked.

"Since I've been working with Caroline and Preston, I thought I might be of some help," she said.

"That is very kind of you," C.B. said. He was like putty in her hands. Alex felt a little jealous.

"Pres owns a couple of companies," C.B. said. "Would you like the names?"

"If you don't mind, that would be very helpful," she said.

Alex gritted his teeth. Yesterday he'd asked his father for other ways to reach Preston and got the runaround. C.B. had insisted on handling everything himself, as usual.

C.B. went to his desk, flipped open a folder lying right on top. Apparently, he'd been trying again to reach *Pres*. "One is a company called Wellington Enterprises."

The same name as the one Caroline had written all the checks to.

"The other is—" C.B. dug through the folder "—Maple Ridge Unlimited."

"Are those companies in Miami?" Samantha was asking.

"Both out of New York," C.B. said with obvious pride. "Pres is quite the young man. Smart and ambitious."

Alex groaned inwardly. Even Brian looked a little green around the gills. Their father admired ambition almost as much as he did money.

As C.B. closed the folder on his desk, Alex had a very bad feeling. "Let me guess, you invested money in Pres's companies."

C.B. shot him a hard look. "You wouldn't presume to advise me on how to invest my money, would you, Alex?"

"What would a fireman know about such things," Alex quipped.

Exactly, his father's look said before the older man moved closer to Samantha and said something Alex didn't catch.

Alex glanced at his brother.

Brian had wandered over to their father's desk and had lifted the corner of the folder from which C.B. had gotten the names of Preston's companies just moments before. Brian appeared to be scanning the information inside the folder.

"Brian, you're awfully quiet tonight," Alex said.

His brother started, letting the folder fall shut as he stepped away from the desk. "I don't speak when I have nothing to say."

Alex groaned at his brother's arrogance. "Oh, I suspect you have plenty to say—behind my back."

"So why did Caroline take you with her yesterday?" Brian asked.

Alex wished he knew. "I guess she wanted one of her brothers with her and I was available."

Brian smirked at that. "One of the benefits of having what amounts to little more than a part-time job. What I don't understand is why you've taken it on yourself to find Preston. I thought Dad told you he had already left a message. What are you trying to prove anyway?"

Alex started to step toward his brother but felt Samantha's cool touch on his arm.

"Thank you for your help," she said in that calming tone of hers. "I know how much Preston would appreciate our efforts to locate him. He will want to be at Caroline's side."

Yeah right, Alex thought as he let her steer him toward the door. He was still fuming when they climbed into his pickup, but he didn't say anything until they were out the gate and he could no longer see the grounds in his rearview mirror.

"THAT WENT WELL," Alex said with a laugh, his large hands gripping the wheel. "Now you see why I give my family a wide berth. But you were great with my father." His gaze met hers and locked for an instant. "You really are amazing." He turned back to his driving but she could still feel the heat of that gaze warming her to her toes.

"You know something good might come out of this,"

he was saying. "This might be just the humbling experience my father and brother need. I have a feeling that my father probably invested a bundle with his future son-in-law *Pres*. And Brian, too." He glanced over at her. "And they're both going to lose it all."

"How can you be so sure of that?"

Alex shook his head. "I hope to hell I'm wrong about *Pres*, but I have a bad feeling we won't be seeing him again."

Samantha considered telling him what she'd found out about Preston Wellington III. But she needed the fingerprints from the champagne bottle and glasses first. She needed to know exactly what they were dealing with before she hit him with the bad news.

And Alex was in enough of a temper as it was. In the mood he was in, he would return to his father's house and slap them with the news that Preston Wellington III didn't even exist. At least not until a year ago.

She didn't want that happening. It would only open a bigger can of worms. A man like C. B. Graham would demand to know how she'd come by such information. She couldn't chance blowing her cover. It would be hard enough to convince Alex.

Alex dropped her off at her office saying he had to go by the firehouse. He was taking some time off.

After he left, Samantha went upstairs to be briefed on the other members parts of the Sonya Botero case.

Unfortunately, there was little news. Julia, who'd been friends with Sonya, had been working to see if there was a connection between any of the people they knew, friends, relatives, acquaintances.

Sophie was working on the Craig Johnson part of the investigation. Isabelle was getting ready to go to Ladera. Nicole was using her background as a private investigator for wealthy clients to follow up on some leads. The rest of the team was beating the bushes as well, making contacts with informants, leaving no stone unturned.

After the briefing, Samantha spent the day finalizing last-minute details for the Holcum-Anders wedding. While not one of the shop's largest or most extravagant, the wedding had been in the planning stages for almost a year now and would culminate in the ceremony tomorrow.

Everything was set but still she went over the details again. Her mind had been wandering all day and wandering in an annoying and worrisome direction: Alex Graham.

Her phone rang, making her jump. For just an instant, she thought it would be Alex and was disappointed when she saw it was an inner-office line.

"I've got more bad news for you," Clare said without preamble. "A woman's body was found this morning in the Miami River. Rachel asked me to let you know. I guess she's gone down there to make the identification if it turns out to be Sonya. She's hoping to spare both Juan and Carlos. Might not even be Sonya, although the description sounds close."

Samantha felt sick. "It can't be her. Why take her only to kill her? They didn't even make a ransom demand."

"Sometimes it isn't about money, you know that."

Hadn't she suspected that if Preston, or whoever he was, was behind this that he'd taken Sonya just to hide his true crime—his attempt on Caroline's life. "Let me know as soon as you hear?"

"I will. And as for Preston Wellington III…"

Samantha braced herself for the worst.

"During the last year he's made a bunch of investments. Looks like he might be overextended. Big-time."

Just as Alex had suspected. "Check something for me?" She hated to even voice her latest fear. "Did he by any chance take out an insurance policy on his future bride?"

ALEX MADE A DOZEN more attempts to reach his sister's fiancé, then did something drastic. He called his brother.

"I'm sorry but Mr. Graham is in a meeting," the third secretary he spoke to told him.

"I don't want to speak with Mr. Graham, I want to speak with Brian. Which secretary are you?" Alex asked.

"I'm his private secretary," the woman said.

"What man needs three secretaries? Look, tell Brian his brother is on the line and if he doesn't take my call I will come down there. It's urgent."

"One moment please."

It wasn't a minute later that Brian came on. "What the hell are you doing threatening my staff?"

"*Three* secretaries?"

"Did you want something? I'm busy."

Alex raked a hand through his hair and sighed. "I still haven't been able to reach Caroline's fiancé."

"That's why you got me out of an important meeting?" He swore. "I told you Dad was handling this."

"Don't you think the man should know that his fiancée is in the hospital, possibly even…" He veered away from even the thought. "I know Dad invested some money with him. He wouldn't have done that without checking with you first." Silence. "Dammit, Brian, if you have some way to reach the man, I want it. And if you don't, I want to know why the hell not."

His brother sighed deeply. "I have the same numbers you do."

"Dad did invest with him, didn't he?"

"I have to get back to my meeting."

"How about addresses then? These businesses *Pres* sold the two of you on, they have addresses, right?"

For a moment, he thought his brother would just hang up on him. Or at the very least refuse to give them to him. "I'll have one of my secretaries find them for you and call you back," Brian said.

"I'll hold." But while he waited Alex realized Brian wouldn't give him the addresses unless Brian had already tried finding Preston through them—and couldn't.

Another dead end.

IT SURPRISED SAMANTHA that she hadn't heard from Alex again. Had something happened? She called the hospital but Caroline was still unconscious.

Maybe Alex had located Preston. He might already know more than she did about his sister's fiancé.

Samantha got up and went to her office window to look out on the bay and was surprised it was dark outside. The shop had been closed all day because of what had happened but the team had still been working—getting ready for the Holcom-Anders wedding tomorrow and trying to find out what had happened to Sonya Botero.

Now, though, the place had taken on an eerie emptiness as she straightened her desk and picked up her purse to leave. She had done everything she could for the wedding tomorrow. She couldn't just sit here but she didn't want to go home, either. She was too anxious waiting to hear about the body that had been found in the river, to hear about Caroline's condition, to hear more news about Preston Wellington III—or whoever he was.

She headed for the door, not completely sure where she was going to go. She had Clare looking into Preston's two companies.

There was no one at the desk. The place looked deserted. She hadn't realized how late it was. She couldn't even be sure there was anyone left upstairs.

For the first time since working here, she felt vulnerable as she walked to her car parked on the side of the building.

Her car, like her and her cover, made a point of not standing out—white, midsize with few bells and whistles. It perfectly fit the Samantha Peters she'd become.

But part of her wanted to take the black sports car and that was the part of her she was worried about as she got into the white sedan and checked the gun in her purse. Now, maybe more than ever, she needed to go unnoticed. Both by whoever had been following her and Alex. But mostly by Alex.

She couldn't shake the feeling she was being watched as she reached into the secret compartment where she kept extra ammunition. She slipped another clip for her gun into her purse along with a small can of pepper spray. She really was feeling paranoid. But better to be safe than sorry. She started the car and pulled out.

This part of town was always busy but she saw no one paying any attention to her. At least not that she could see. But that didn't mean anything.

As she pulled away from the shop, she watched to see if she was followed. She didn't see a tail but she couldn't shake the feeling that someone had taken even more interest in her after last night—an interest that now was deadly.

She almost hoped she would pick up the tail as she drove around aimlessly for a good fifteen minutes before heading for the hospital. Whoever had tailed her and Alex last night had to be tied to Sonya Botero's abduction or Caroline Graham's hit-and-run. Or both, if they were connected. If she could catch whoever had been following her and Alex at least the team might get some answers.

But she saw no one following her. Unfortunately, at this hour of the day, there were too many cars, making it easy for the tail to go unnoticed.

After parking in the visitors section at the hospital, she tried Preston Wellington III's phone number again. No answer. As futile as she feared it was, she left another message.

Inside the empty elevator, she pushed the button for Caroline Graham's floor and leaned back against the wall, her thoughts scattered in a hundred different directions. She had to tell Alex what she'd learned about Preston Wellington III. She knew he would be even more suspicious of how she'd come by the information and that worried her.

But her biggest concern at this point was Caroline. If her fiancé had tried to kill her—

The elevator door opened and she stepped off on Caroline's floor. The nurses' station was empty.

The guard outside Caroline's room was busy reading a book. He didn't even look up. Samantha stuck her head into Caroline's room. She was sleeping.

The hallway was so quiet she heard the faint creak of a door opening as she neared Craig Johnson's room.

A doctor in surgical garb had come out of the stairwell. He didn't even look in her direction as he stepped into Craig Johnson's room.

Samantha stood for a moment, trying to pinpoint what was bothering her about the doctor. Why was he dressed in surgical garb and wandering around the hospital? And why had he gone into Johnson's room? Johnson didn't need a surgeon.

Had Craig Johnson been right to fear for his life?

Chapter Eight

As the surgeon disappeared into Craig Johnson's room, Samantha quickened her step, all the time telling herself she was mistaken. She wasn't thinking clearly. Why else had she let her guard down with Alex Graham?

At the door to Johnson's room, she hesitated, then throwing caution to the wind, she burst in.

She heard a clatter and saw at once why. Someone had wedged one of the chairs under the knob. But the chair hadn't held on the slick floor. It skittered across the linoleum to crash into the wall.

Past it, she saw the doctor. He was struggling to hold the patient down, one arm locked around Johnson's throat, the other clutching a hypodermic needle. Johnson was bucking on the bed, his face already turning blue, the hypodermic needle dripping a clear liquid.

At the sight of Samantha, Johnson's eyes bulged. He opened his mouth but no sound came out.

The doctor had spun around at the sound of the chair

clattering to the floor. Samantha had her hand in her bag, but instead of her fingers closing around the gun, she felt the small can of pepper spray.

She brought it out, but the man moved too quickly. He released Johnson and launched himself at her, the hypodermic needle raised in the air.

She brought up the can of pepper spray, her finger fumbling for the button, as he grabbed for her. The spray caught him in the face. He let out of a howl of pain, now groping blindly for her.

She stepped out of his reach to grab up the overturned chair, swinging it at him with one hand. It caught him in the knees. He stumbled and almost fell, catching himself awkwardly as he tripped and banged into the wall.

He let out an oath and wiped frantically at his eyes with the sleeve of the surgical gown. His face was beet-red, his eyes running with tears, but his gaze found her.

Her hand was shaking as she groped in her bag, this time coming up with the gun. She leveled it at him, ready to fire.

He reached down and before she could fire, hurled the chair at her. She ducked but it caught her in the shoulder and knocked her back. She hit the floor hard, coming down on her butt, the gun still in her hand, though.

Not that it mattered.

The imposter doctor was gone. The door closing behind him.

She struggled to get up, her limbs like water, her shoulder aching. This was the second time she'd been hit in two days. She felt out of her league, in pain and frustrated.

Hurrying to the door, she looked out. The hallway was empty. The man was gone.

Turning she looked to the bed and Craig Johnson. He appeared scared as hell but alive.

"Are you all right?" she asked, realizing he hadn't hit the call button for a nurse. Nor had he picked up the phone and called the police while she'd been trying to save his life or jumped in to help her. She felt a wave of anger wash through her as she moved to the bed.

Johnson was sitting up in the bed, rubbing his throat, color coming back into his face as he sucked in deep breaths.

She stepped to the call button, but he grabbed her hand before she could push it.

"I'm all right," he said hoarsely.

"That man tried to kill you."

Johnson gave her a look that said he knew that better than she did.

"Why would he want you dead?" she demanded.

"How should I know?"

"Because it has something to do with Sonya Botero's abduction."

Johnson shook his head. "It is a private matter."

"We need to call the police."

"No. It is my business alone."

She didn't believe him. "If this has something to do with Sonya Botero's abduction—"

"It is gambling debts. What do you care anyway?" He was eyeing her with suspicion. "You are that wedding planner and yet you carry pepper spray and a gun?"

"Any woman who's smart and lives and works in Miami does," she shot back.

"Stay out of my business, wedding planner."

"I just saved your life. I would think you would be more grateful."

"It isn't the first time someone has tried to kill me for the money I owe. Nor will it be the last time."

"Sounds like a motive for kidnapping someone like Sonya Botero," Samantha said.

His eyes narrowed. "You don't want to get involved in this."

"I got involved when I saved your life."

"Your mistake," Johnson said and closed his eyes. "Now get out of my room and if you call the police I will deny everything."

"Yes," she said tamping down the urge to shoot him herself. "You are very good at denying everything."

He didn't open his eyes. Nor did he respond. She checked to make sure she had her gun and her pepper spray. Her eyes were burning from what little she'd sprayed as she left the room, letting the door close behind her.

Out in the hall, she took deep breaths of air and let her watering eyes clear. Then carefully she opened the door to Johnson's room a crack and listened.

Just as she'd suspected, he was on the phone.

"The bastards tried to kill me again!" he said, his whisper shrill. "Do something." He slammed down the phone.

Samantha eased the door closed and walked down to the elevator. She was still a little wobbly on her feet, still shaken, her eyes still burning. Changing her mind, she headed for the outdoor terrace at the end of the hallway.

It wasn't until she'd dialed Rachel's cell that she noticed she had a message from her. Rachel answered on the first ring as if she'd been expecting a call.

"The body in the river? Was it Sonya?" Samantha asked quietly.

"No."

Samantha leaned against the garden wall, relief and the aftereffects of her latest encounter with a killer, making her weak. She thought about the dead woman. Some other family and friends would be grieving tonight.

"Are you all right?" Rachel asked. "You sound funny."

"I'm at the hospital. Someone just tried to kill Sonya's chauffer. I didn't get a good look at the man. All I know is that he was Hispanic, medium height and weight, no visible scars or tattoos. He was wearing a surgical mask, posing as a doctor. Johnson refused to let me call the police. He says it has to do with gambling debts."

"So he needed money," Rachel said. "I'll have the team see if he's telling the truth. Are you sure you're all right?"

"A few new bruises, nothing serious." Her shoulder ached. All she wanted to do was go home to her hot tub, pour herself some wine and soak. "He placed another call after I saved his life and he kicked me out of his room without even a thank-you."

Rachel let out a long breath. "We got the number Johnson called before. It's a pay phone in Ladera. He has family ties there so it proves nothing. We'll see where he called this time and keep an eye on him. I thought there was a guard down the hall in front of Caroline Graham's door?"

"He was reading and not paying any attention," Samantha said. "No reason he would. The guy looked like a doctor in all that surgical garb and he didn't try to go into Caroline's room. Johnson's running scared, but even so, he isn't talking."

"And Caroline Graham?" Rachel asked.

"Still unconscious. I'm going to go home now."

"Good idea. By the way, nice work." Rachel hung up.

Samantha stuffed her phone back in her purse and headed for the elevator, glad to see it was empty. She hit the lobby button, closed her eyes and leaned back against the cool surface of the wall.

All she wanted was to be out of this hospital and in her car headed home. She really wished she'd brought the sports car now. She could make it home much faster.

The elevator doors started to close.

Her eyes flew open as she heard someone slam the elevator doors open again.

Chapter Nine

Alex was startled to see Samantha. Almost as startled as she was. He saw her hand go to her purse and for an instant he thought she was going for a gun.

He half laughed at how crazy that thought was. A wedding planner with a gun?

But was that any crazier than some of the more personal thoughts he'd been having about her?

"Well, hello." He couldn't believe how happy he was to see her.

She, however, didn't look all that happy to see him. She looked…guilty of something. He'd already suspected that Samantha was hiding something from him. Now he was almost positive of it.

He decided what he needed to do was keep an eye on her. He smiled at the thought. It really was no hardship. The woman was easy to look at. And she already intrigued him. And any excuse would do to get closer to her.

"Were you visiting someone in the hospital?" he asked, watching color flood back into her face as he held the elevator door so it didn't close. She released the death grip she had on her purse and straightened.

He realized he'd caught her at a rare moment. Had this prim and proper woman actually been leaning against the back of the elevator resting and he'd startled her?

He recalled the other time he'd startled her and wondered again what had happened to her that made her fearful. A man, he thought with some clarity. That might explain the way she dressed. This woman didn't want to attract attention.

Her hair swung back from her face and he saw the bruise and cut he'd seen earlier when he'd come by her office and talked her into going with him to his father's. She'd said she banged into something being clumsy. Even at the time he couldn't imagine her ever being clumsy.

He suspected there was another story—one much more interesting that she wasn't telling him. Nothing new there.

"I was worried about your sister," she said and stepped toward the door as if to escape. "I just came up to see how she was doing."

"Really?" His heart beat a little faster. "Then you know she's conscious." He could tell by her expression she hadn't heard. Had he caught her in a lie? Possibly not her first. He suspected she'd been down the hall visiting the chauffeur again. More eavesdropping?

"She was sleeping so I didn't know she'd regained consciousness. That's wonderful news." He could hear

Samantha's obvious relief that Caroline was alive and getting better. While he didn't understand this woman, something told him that whatever she might be up to, she was one of the good guys. At least he hoped to hell that was true because he felt something for her. Something he hadn't felt in a long time for a woman.

But then he had a track record for falling in love with the wrong woman. Usually one he couldn't trust, he reminded himself.

"Did you get to talk to Caroline?" she asked.

"The doctor let me see her for a few moments. She's pretty out of it still."

"So you didn't ask about Preston."

He shook his head as he let the elevator doors go and stepped in. She'd already pushed the ground floor button. "No reason to hit her with any of that the moment she wakes up, right?"

Samantha nodded and smiled. "I'm sure once she's able she'll clear this all up."

Right. "Any word on that other woman?" he asked.

She shook her head.

The elevator doors opened on the ground floor. He told himself that he couldn't let her get away—maybe even more so because she looked as if that's exactly what she wanted to do.

"I still can't believe it but the doctor says Caroline and the baby are going to be fine. Don't you think this calls for a celebration?"

Instantly, she started to decline.

"Just one drink. Please. I can't tell you how relieved I am, but then I suspect I don't have to."

"No, you don't." He could see that she was weakening.

"Just one drink to celebrate this good news."

"All right." She seemed different. It took him a moment to put his finger on what it was. She was always in control. Except tonight. Tonight there was a vulnerability to her. He felt a pull toward her like the force of gravity. He wanted to take her in his arms and hold her, protect her, comfort her.

"Still no word from Preston?" she asked giving him the impression she was just trying to make conversation since he would have told her if he'd heard anything.

He shook his head. "I think Preston probably used Caroline to get to my father. I'm not sure how much money C.B. gave Preston but I have a bad feeling it was considerable." He told her that his brother, Brian, had provided him with the addresses of Preston's supposed businesses. They had proved worthless, just as Alex had suspected.

Samantha Peters looked sick. "I can't imagine what this will do to Caroline."

"I still think he's behind what happened to her. So, one way or another, I'll find him and get to the truth."

THAT WAS WHAT SAMANTHA was afraid of—that Alex was the kind of man that settled for nothing less than the truth.

It was one reason she felt so jumpy. That and almost being killed earlier upstairs in Craig Johnson's room. That and the intimacy of being in this elevator alone with

Alex. That and the fact that she was lying to this man. Not lying exactly, but definitely not being honest with him.

And what made it all the worse was that he didn't realize how dangerous the situation had become. She had to warn him, had to tell him everything she knew. It was the only reason she'd agreed to have a drink with him. At least that's what she told herself. She would tell him everything. Well, enough that he would stop his investigation of Preston Wellington III or whoever the man was. She couldn't live with herself if anything happened to Alex.

As they stepped off on the ground floor, Alex reached over and touched her hand.

She felt a jolt of warmth and did her best not to react.

"I'll get my truck. Wait here." He didn't give her a chance to argue. She watched him walk away, no wasted effort, his body lean and strong, the man himself self-confident. She felt a pull so strong that she couldn't look away and chastised herself for wanting to watch Alex for those few moments longer before he disappeared into the darkness of the parking lot.

He had struck a chord in her and she didn't know what she was going to do about it. She'd tried fighting her feelings for all the good it had done. She felt excited and scared and had to remind herself that Alex Graham didn't know who she was. And when he did—

He drove up in his pickup and smiled at her as she stepped out into the humid night air. She could feel him watching her. Looking for something? Or just looking? She feared either way that ultimately he would be disappointed.

FOR THE SECOND TIME, Alex sensed there was something she wanted to say but had stopped herself as she climbed into the truck.

"Something on your mind?" he asked as he drove.

She touched her upper lip with her tongue. "I need to tell you something."

"Okay," he said slowly. "You're going to kill me but first…I'm starved and I'm willing to bet you haven't had a thing to eat all day. I know this place that serves the best marinara sauce you've ever tasted. It's not far from here and we can have the celebratory drink."

"You're always feeding me," she said, sounding a little embarrassed.

"I like to eat and I hate to eat alone." He didn't add that he liked to see her eat. Or that she looked better since he'd started feeding her. "Great, then," he said and reached over to squeeze her hand as he drove toward the restaurant. He felt her start, tension jumping just under her skin.

He picked up a small buzz of electricity himself when he touched her, but his was attraction. He feared that hers was something entirely different.

VICTOR CONSTANTINE made the call the minute he saw them come out of the hospital. Alex Graham and the wedding planner, Samantha Peters, crossed to the parking lot and got into Graham's pickup. He'd broken his number-one rule. He'd found out who he was following.

"They just left the hospital." Probably to visit Alex's sister, Caroline Graham. He'd made a point of finding that out, too. Just as he had found out who the woman was with Alex Graham. Caroline Graham had regained consciousness. He wondered if his client knew that. Or cared.

Victor couldn't help but wonder what his client's stake was in all this. It was a first time for him, wondering. Worth doing some investigating on his own. He was looking forward to breaking into Samantha Peters's house once he got her address. Her, he was very curious about.

It should have worried him more that he'd broken his own rules. But he told himself this was his last job. Why not indulge his curiosity?

"Follow them. Maybe we'll get lucky tonight and find out where the woman lives. That is, if you don't lose her again."

Victor said nothing. There was nothing he could say. His client didn't even know that he'd lost her not once but twice.

Tonight he would be more careful. Tonight, he would be ready for her. But even as he thought it, he wasn't sure that would help.

THE ITALIAN CAFÉ was small and intimate and just perfect for a romantic evening—or a place to talk to Samantha Peters and find out what she was hiding.

But at the same time, he knew that once she told him it was going to change things. He wasn't sure he was ready for that.

"Romano," Alex said cheerfully as he greeted the owner.

The large Italian clasped his hand warmly. "Alex, so nice to see you and who do you have here?" He released Alex's hand to take both of Samantha's in his. He said in Italian, "She looks like you've been starving her. But not to worry. I will fatten her up."

"Fattening up is the last thing I need," Samantha answered in perfect Italian.

Alex stared at her in surprise. Samantha Peters was just full of surprises, wasn't she?

Romano laughed heartily, warming to her even more. "I have just the thing for you. I'll have my chef make it special." He let go of her hands and touched his lips with his fingertips in a kiss.

"You speak Italian," Alex said.

"As do you," she said in Italian.

He smiled over at her. "A nice quiet booth in the back?" he said to Romano, although never taking his eyes off Samantha. The woman never ceased to amaze him.

The café owner led them back through the narrow room, past red-and-white-checked tablecloths, glowing candles and tall wooden booths draped with brightly colored curtains.

Samantha slid into the booth and looked around, seeming uncomfortable, as if she felt out of place. As he sat down across from her, he wondered if she was sorry she'd revealed a little more of herself by acknowledging that she understood Italian.

Candlelight flickered warmly over her face and with a stab of desire, he realized that she'd never looked more beautiful than she did tonight.

She must have felt his eyes on her. She brushed a lock of brown hair from behind her ear and let it fall so it hid part of her face again.

She picked up her menu. "All I really need is a salad…."

Alex laughed. "Trust me you are not getting out of here that easy. Romano would not allow it."

"Really, Alex—"

"What are you afraid of?" he asked, leaning across the table toward her.

A wary look leaped to her eyes.

"It's only food," he said smiling at her. "One of many fun indulgences I have a feeling you've been missing out on." Her cheeks flamed. Was she actually *blushing?* "I'm sorry, I didn't mean to embarrass you."

He leaned back as a young Italian waiter put down a basket of warm, savory-smelling bread, a small bowl of whipped fresh creamery butter and a bottle of wine and two glasses. "Compliments of the house," the waiter said with a bow.

"I'm not even going to pretend I know anything about wine," Alex said to Samantha and laughed, hoping to relieve some of her tension. She looked ready to spring out of her booth and run. "I can only assume it's a very good year, given that Romano is obviously trying to impress you."

The waiter uncorked the wine—Alex waved away the offer to smell the cork—and poured them both a glass and left.

Alex raised his glass in a toast and realized he didn't want to talk about Caroline, her fiancé, anything that might spoil this moment. And just maybe there was an even better way to find out about this woman. "Tonight let's just enjoy ourselves. I really want to forget about *everything* and just enjoy your fascinating company. Whatever it is you want to talk to me about, I'm sure it can wait. Indulge me this one night?"

INDULGING ALEX GRAHAM? That's the last thing she wanted to do, she thought as she reluctantly touched her wineglass to his. She'd seen his appetite for food. Was keenly aware of his appetite for life. As a fireman, she knew the man enjoyed taking chances, living on the edge—the exact opposite of Samantha Peters.

Being this near him she couldn't just feel his enormous energy, it seemed to infuse her with the desire to not only indulge him, but herself.

She took a sip of her wine, her hand shaking, and tried to concentrate on something else. The music. An Italian love song. Alex was looking at her with that intensity that warned her he saw beneath the surface. He saw what she had been so successful at keeping a secret for years.

He got to his feet and reached for her hand. "Dance with me."

Before she could decline, he had drawn her up and into his arms, whirling her expertly onto the small dance floor she hadn't noticed before. She saw Romano smiling at them from the shadows and suspected he'd intentionally played the song. He gave her a wink.

She tried to relax. Being in Alex's arms was heaven. And hell.

"You dance very well," he said, holding her close as they moved to the sensuous beat of the music.

She was intensely aware of the places his body touched hers. The smell of his light aftershave and distinct male scent filled her senses, making her dizzy in a way the wine never would have.

She felt both relief and disappointment when the song ended and he led her back to the table, releasing her hand as he slid into the booth across from her.

The food arrived in a flurry of dishes and aromas. Alex was like a kid in a candy store and she felt herself being swept up by his enthusiasm.

He began to explain each of Romano's specialties as he spooned them onto her plate. She listened, enjoying the sound of his voice as much as the smell of the food.

He waited for her to taste each one.

She indulged him—and herself. Obediently, she tried a bite of each one, giving the appropriate responses all of which met with a smile from Alex. "This is *wonderful*," she said with a wave of her hand.

He laughed as he refilled her wineglass.

They ate and drank, laughing and joking. The meal, the music, the warmth of the café and each other totally relaxed her.

Just for tonight, she told herself, watching Alex savor each bite, each sip of wine, each laugh they shared, she would let herself enjoy this. Enjoy Alex. Just for this magical, wonderful tonight.

ALEX WAS SMILING at something Samantha had said when he saw from the corner of his eye someone approaching their booth.

He glanced up and saw the last person he wanted to see. "Brian?" He'd never seen him here before.

"Looks like the two of you have been enjoying yourselves." Brian picked up one of the two empty wine bottles on the table.

Alex hadn't realized they'd drunk that much. Nor had he realized how late it was. They'd been here for hours. He'd been having too much fun to notice.

"We were just leaving," Alex said to his brother, amazed how quickly the tone of their dinner had changed when wet-blanket Brian appeared.

"You've both had too much to drink for either of you to drive," Brian said.

Alex started to argue that he didn't need Brian telling him what to do.

"I insist," Brian said, a little less abrasively. "Please, let my driver take you both home. Can you let me do this one small thing for you? I am your brother." Brian seemed to have had a little to drink himself and appeared sincere. Alex figured Brian was just trying to impress Samantha. And it seemed to be working.

"It's a gracious offer," Samantha, the peacekeeper, said and looked to Alex as if she thought Brian was trying to be kind.

"Be gracious for once," Brian said quietly.

Alex didn't want to make a scene and truthfully, he had drunk a lot of wine and so had Samantha. He'd planned to call a cab for them, but why not take Brian's limo and driver and let Brian take a cab.

"Sure," Alex said with a smile. "Whatever the lady wants."

Samantha gave him a thankful smile. The woman actually thought she could make peace in the Graham family? Her optimism was one of the things Alex found so delightful about her.

Alex watched Brian pick up their bill. "I'll get this," Brian said and smiled at Samantha. Yep, his brother was just trying to impress her. "Good night." Brian turned and walked back to a booth down the aisle. Alex couldn't see who he was sitting with.

The limo driver leaped out to open their doors the moment they came out of the restaurant. Alex realized that Brian had called the driver, no doubt with instructions.

Alex tried to be gracious even though he found a limo and driver too pretentious, not to mention the inside of Brian's limo.

"Pretty impressive," Alex said as he sank down next to Samantha on the deep warm leather seat. He had a wayward thought. Why was Brian going out of his way to impress Samantha? Did he think Alex and Samantha were an item and wanted to steal Samantha away?

He felt a stab of jealousy. And more than a little concern. Could Samantha be taken in by Brian's success, his lifestyle, his money?

Alex glanced over at her as the limo driver asked for Samantha's address. She gave it and the driver put up the thick glass between him and the back.

Samantha was gazing around the inside of the most expensive limo that money could buy. She *was* impressed, Alex thought.

He couldn't help himself. "You do realize that my brother has an ulterior motive."

She cut her eyes to him and seemed disappointed that he was looking a gift horse in the mouth.

"Trust me, my brother is up to something," Alex persisted.

"Maybe he really was just being nice," she suggested.

Alex laughed and shook his head. "Brian doesn't do things just to be nice. You can bet there's something in it for him."

But what Brian didn't know was that Alex was willing to fight for this woman. He might not have all the things that his brother did, including a prestigious job and a cool limo, but Alex did have something to offer this woman.

He put his arm around her. She turned to regard him. He'd expected surprise. Or at least the usual wariness.

Instead it was almost as if she wanted this as much as he did. Almost as if she'd been expecting his kiss.

VICTOR COULDN'T believe his luck. There was no way he was going to lose this fancy-pants limo, not in a million years. And unless he missed his guess the driver was going to lead him right to Samantha Peters's house.

This was finally working out. He thought about calling his client and telling him the good news.

But even as he thought it, he knew he wasn't going to tell his client. Another broken rule of his. Withholding information from a client.

Victor felt a rush of expectation. He'd been following this woman all over Miami. Finally he would get a look at her house. Not to mention, she would be home.

He felt a tightness in his belly. Normally, he didn't desire women. But this one... This one was different. And he did like to take his passion by force on occasion.

Yes, he would break every rule tonight.

This would definitely be his last job.

He would end it with Samantha Peters.

Chapter Ten

The kiss was everything Samantha knew it would be. His mouth was warm and soft at first, tentative then insistent.

She'd wanted it, wanted him, wanted to feel his lips on hers. He was strong, his chest rock hard, and yet there was a tenderness about the way he held her, the way he kissed her.

At first.

Then he drew her closer until her breasts were crushed against his chest, her nipples as hard as pebbles and aching.

Desire raced along her nerve endings, heating her blood, quickening her pulse. She felt need rush to her center. Her breath came faster.

He deepened the kiss, the tip of his tongue brushing over hers. She felt a quiver of excitement as he shifted in the seat so his hand could cup her breast. His fingers brushed over the turgid nipple and she quaked at his touch, a soft moan escaping her lips.

They were completely alone. Nothing could stop them from making love.

Samantha knew *she* should stop him. Stop herself. Nothing good could come of this. It was wrong in every way, given that he was part of a case she was working on. And she was lying to him about who she really was. Not to mention that he would end up hurting her. That was a given, wasn't it?

But she wanted him as she'd never wanted any man. She told herself that if she could have him just for tonight it would be enough—no matter what the future held. She lied to herself because right now she couldn't have stopped him if her life had depended on it.

He pulled her skirt up until he could reach under it. She felt his hand between her legs. He cupped her there through her panties and she pushed against him, needing him inside her.

His cell phone rang. He ignored it as he began to open the button of her suit jacket, his fingers working hurriedly as if, like her, he couldn't wait to bare her breasts to his touch, to his lips, to his tongue.

The cell phone rang again.

She groaned and arched against him as his left hand cupped her breast and the other finished unbuttoning first her suit jacket, then her silk blouse down to the lacy black bra she wore.

She heard his intake of air as he saw the bra, saw the smooth white curve of her abundant cleavage, the nipples pressing against the sheer black fabric. His nimble fingers unhooked the front latch freeing her breasts.

He let out a groan as he dropped his head down to suckle at one, then the other.

He was working her skirt up, his hand snaking under her panties when the phone rang again.

With a curse he drew back and reached for it as if to turn it off. His glance fell on the caller ID and he swore again, his gaze coming to hers.

"It says caller unknown, could be the hospital. I have to take this," he said.

She nodded when what she really wanted to do was scream. But the call might be about Caroline. Of course he had to take it.

She pulled down her skirt and drew her blouse over her breasts even though Alex had turned away from her, the side windows were tinted and there was only darkness outside, and she couldn't see the driver through the privacy screen.

She placed a hand on Alex's broad back, not wanting to break the connection between them and closed her eyes, the ache painful. She could still feel his mouth on her breasts. She was wet with need for this man. It had been so long and no man had ever made her feel like this.

She felt him tense under her hand and opened her eyes, knowing it was bad news. Slowly she removed her hand from his back and began to button up her blouse, then her jacket.

FOR A FEW MOMENTS, Alex thought he hadn't heard the caller correctly. The voice on the other end of the line was disguised. It threw Alex for a moment.

He'd assumed that the call was from the hospital and had taken it expecting it to be a doctor. Or maybe Preston calling about Caroline.

Instead it had been the strange-sounding voice. The words even stranger.

"Thought you'd like to know that your girlfriend broke into your sister's condo last night. Now why would a wedding planner do that?"

"What?" he'd asked, sitting up straighter. He no longer felt Samantha's hand on his back.

"Why don't you ask your girlfriend if you don't believe me. Ask her how she got that bruise on her cheek."

The line went dead.

Alex sat holding the phone, the caller's words finally starting to register. His girlfriend? Samantha? He glanced back at her. She'd dressed again.

"Bad news?" she asked, looking scared. "Is Caroline all right?"

He nodded. "It was just...just a crank call." Or was it? He tried to imagine Samantha in her business suit breaking into anyone's condo let alone Caroline's in that not-so-fine part of town.

Anyway, she couldn't have gotten past the guard.

Or maybe she could, he thought as he recalled her defensive reaction when he'd come up behind her at the hospital.

So she had some self-defense training. But that didn't make her a woman who committed B and Es.

For a moment he thought about asking her. But what would he say? "Break into any condos lately?"

That was just plain crazy.

What possible reason would she have to go back to the condo, let alone break in? None.

He sat back, disappointed because the moment was lost. The driver tapped on the security screen. Alex hit the button, the separator coming down.

"We've reached your guest's residence," the driver said.

Alex looked out at the beach house. Nice location. This hadn't come cheap. He wondered what wedding planners made and hated that he was even more suspicious of a woman he would have made love to if it hadn't been for the call.

SOMETHING HAD CHANGED. Samantha could see it in his eyes. If Caroline was all right, then what had the call been about? Whatever it was, Alex didn't seem to want to tell her.

The interruption had definitely sobered them both up. The driver opened her door.

"I'll be right back," Alex said as he slid out and walked her to her front door. Apparently he wasn't coming in.

She felt as if she'd been saved—and hated every moment of it. "Thank you for tonight."

He smiled at that. "It didn't go the way I had hoped."

"Maybe some other time," she said brazenly.

"Maybe," he said with a nod as he leaned toward her. It was a goodbye kiss and it took every ounce of her strength not to put her arms around him and pull him down for a real kiss.

But by then he had turned and was walking back to the limo.

She opened her front door and stepped inside, not having the strength to watch him walk away. Who had the call been from? Whoever it was had changed things instantly. Another woman?

The thought almost floored her. Of course a man like Alex Graham would have a lover. How foolish of her not to realize that.

Suddenly she felt the ache in her shoulder, the fatigue of the last two days, and yet she knew sleep would never come. Not tonight. Not after what had almost happened.

She walked through the house, not bothering to turn on a light and went straight to the garage. The motorcycle was a crotch-rocket, the fastest, sleekest one that money could buy. She didn't even bother changing her clothes as she lifted her skirt and swung a leg over the leather seat and snugged down her helmet.

The moment she heard the limo drive away, she hit the garage door opener and the door began to rise. She didn't wait for it to reach the top before she shot out, signaling the door to close automatically as she took the first corner and sped toward her office.

She passed the limo going eighty-five. Even if Alex had looked over, he wouldn't have recognized her, she told herself. His mind would be on the woman who'd called him. If indeed it had been a woman. He was probably on his way to her house.

Samantha pushed the bike up to a hundred, trying just as hard to push Alex Graham from her mind. Tonight should have taught her something. Not to make the same mistakes she had in the past with men.

ALEX COULDN'T GET the call out of his mind. He knew he wouldn't be able to sleep. Was it possible that the caller had been Preston?

Maybe Preston was just trying to get him over to Caroline's condo again tonight. Could it be a trap of some sort?

That made even less sense than Samantha going back over to the condo last night and breaking in.

The driver had put the window up between them. Alex touched the intercom button. "Drop me back at the restaurant so I can pick up my truck."

The driver nodded. "Whatever you say, sir."

Alex realized, a little belatedly, that the driver would be reporting to Brian. Alex wasn't sure what bothered him more, that the driver would know hanky-panky was going on in the back during the ride—or that Alex hadn't even tried to spend the night with Samantha.

That, he realized, was the least of his worries, though. If the caller was right about Samantha going back to the condo last night…

It would be just his luck to start falling for another woman he couldn't trust.

VICTOR COULD NOT believe his luck. His bad luck, that is. He'd followed the limo straight to Samantha Peters's door, staying back enough not to be conspicuous.

Everything had been going his way. Alex Graham had kissed her at the door and left. The guy had to be a loser. Even from a distance, Victor could see that the woman was ripe and ready.

Victor couldn't wait for Graham and the limo to leave. Breaking into the place would be child's play for him. He was debating whether to wait until she was asleep or to surprise her now when the garage door opened and a motorcycle came shooting out.

It was her. There was no mistake about it. She was still wearing that awful oversize suit but it was hiked up her slim bare thighs as she zoomed past.

Victor had thought he couldn't want this woman more. He was wrong.

He hurriedly swung his car around and started after her, angry with her that she'd disappointed him more than she could ever know tonight.

But he hadn't gone far when he realized there was no way he was going to catch her. Instead, he fell behind the limo. It was little consolation, but at least he would see where Alex Graham was headed.

ALEX GRAHAM stopped to tell the security guard he needed to get something from his sister's condo again.

"How's she doing if you don't mind me asking?" the guard asked.

"Better. She's conscious."

"Oh, I'm glad to hear that. She's a real nice woman. And her fiancé, too. He never fails to ask about my wife and kids."

Alex thanked the man, surprised by his concern and what he'd said about Caroline's fiancé.

"Have you seen Mr. Wellington around lately?"

The guard shook his head. "He has a lot of irons in the fire so he comes and goes a lot." There was respect and admiration in the man's voice. Alex nodded, thinking Preston certainly fooled a lot of people.

"One more thing," Alex said. "Has anyone else been around the condo since I saw you last night?"

"Not that I know of." The guard looked worried. "Is there a problem?"

"No," Alex said quickly to reassure him. The guard obviously took his job seriously and clearly didn't want to let Preston or Caroline down.

Alex dug out a card with his number on it. "If you see Preston before I do, would you give me a call?"

The guard took the card. "Of course. Tell your sister she's in my prayers."

"I'll do that."

Alex couldn't get the man off his mind as he headed for Caroline's building. His footfalls echoed as he entered. He noticed no sign of a break-in. Taking the elevator, he rode up to Caroline's rooftop condo.

The empty building had an eerie feel to it as he stepped off on her floor. He shone the flashlight he'd brought on the door to her condo but could see no signs that the door had been forced open. For all he knew someone could be waiting inside for him.

If his caller had been telling the truth, how had Samantha gotten in? The caller's story seemed even more outlandish and he wondered what the hell he was doing here this late at night on an obvious wild-goose chase.

He inserted the key and hesitated, hefting the weighty flashlight, as he slowly opened the door. It was dark inside the condo but a little light from the streetlamps outside bled through the plastic.

He turned on the light. Nothing looked any different than it had earlier.

That was until he stepped deeper into the room. A piece of two-by-four lay in the middle of the hallway. He frowned, sure it hadn't been there earlier.

Stepping over it, he started toward the wall of plastic and stopped. Part of the plastic was torn from where it had originally been tacked along the ceiling to keep the dust out of the bedroom.

He stared at the floor. He couldn't swear to it, but there appeared to be more tracks in the Sheetrock dust.

Taking a step back, he picked up the two-by-four and shifted the flashlight to his left hand as he thought about the call he'd received. The caller had known that he and Samantha had been here last night. How? Had they been followed?

Cautiously, he slipped through the opening in the plastic and saw that the bedroom door stood open. He'd made a point of closing it the last time he and Samantha had been here. He gripped the board and flashlight and stepped toward the bedroom.

At first glance, everything looked the same as he remembered it. But then he'd been so upset about his discovery that his sister was pregnant, he wouldn't swear to anything. Just the thought of her celebrating it in this room…

His gaze went to the nightstand beside the bed. The champagne bottle and glasses were gone. His heart began to beat a little faster. He glanced toward the bathroom, expecting to see his reflection in the large mirror just as he had earlier.

Instead, he saw only fragments of himself—and what was left of the mirror.

"What the hell?" He reached for the bathroom light. He'd lived in Miami long enough to recognize a bullet in a wall. There were two in this one, most of the mirror shards on the floor.

He looked around for blood, thankful he didn't see any. What had happened here last night? And why hadn't the guard seen—or heard something?

Because the guard patrolled the entire complex. No doubt whoever had been here had known about the guard and made a point of avoiding him.

Samantha knew about the guard, Alex reminded himself. So did Preston Wellington III.

Alex swore and snapped open his cell phone, but as he started to punch in 911, he stopped. The caller had said the wedding planner had been here.

Someone sure as hell had.

If he called the police he'd have to tell them what little he knew—which was next to nothing. The police were already investigating the abduction of that other woman—and Caroline's hit-and-run.

If he told the police about the call he'd received, they'd question Samantha and probably get nothing. Either way, they wouldn't tell him what they'd learned— just as they hadn't about Caroline's hit-and-run.

No, he thought, putting his cell phone away and thinking about the interlude in the back of the limo tonight. He wanted a shot at Samantha Peters first. If she was involved in this, he would damn well find out.

WHEN SAMANTHA REACHED the office, she wasn't surprised to find Clare working late again, along with several other agents.

"I was just going to call you," Clare said. She didn't look happy. More bad news.

Well, that was the way the night seemed to be going.

"I just got the fingerprint analysis results from the champagne bottle and one of the glasses you sent in last night tagged Urgent," Clare said.

Samantha held her breath. The fact that Clare had gotten results this quickly meant that Preston Wellington III's fingerprints were on file. It was looking more and more as if Alex was right—and she was dead wrong about the man. What a surprise.

"The prints belong to a man named Presley Wells,"

Clare said with a lift of one eyebrow. "Preston Welling-ton III. Presley Wells. You think?"

Samantha groaned. She felt sick. Alex had been right. The names were too similar for there to be any mistake.

Still she held out hope, telling herself he could have changed his name for all kinds of reasons. And his prints could be on file because of a job—not because he had a police record. "He have a record?"

"More than a few problems as a juvenile, but only one arrest as an adult," Clare said. "A burglary. Served some time in Tennessee."

"Tennessee?" Samantha echoed, growing sicker at this news. Alex had been right to worry.

"Tennessee. That's where he was born," Clare said. "I thought you might want an address for his next of kin. His mother is still alive and living outside the town where he was born."

Samantha took down the information. She couldn't keep this from Alex. She was tempted to call him, inter-rupt whatever he had going on tonight, with the bad news.

But she feared she would hear a woman's voice in the background and it would make her feel even worse than she did right now.

She thanked Clare and went back to her office.

She'd been wrong about another man. She was batting a thousand.

Chapter Eleven

The next morning in her office Samantha tried to keep her thoughts on her work, namely the Holcom-Anders wedding.

She went through her list of to-dos and even double-checked the weather channel to make sure there would be no surprises.

The Holcom-Anders wedding was being held on the beach today—one of those huge unpredictable outdoor weddings that drove wedding planners crazy.

With indoor weddings at least you could control the environment. But beach destination weddings were the big thing this year so most of the Holcom clan had flown in several days before and been up in Orlando doing the Disney thing before the wedding. The Anders part of the family had Miami connections so many of the guests would be driving down to Key Largo today.

The weatherman promised sunny skies. Satisfied there was nothing more she could do, Samantha gathered her things and went down to the parking garage to meet the rest of the team for the van ride to Key Largo.

She hadn't seen or heard from Alex since last night. She'd been disappointed when she'd returned home after working as long as she could only to find no message on her machine. She'd promised herself she wouldn't let what almost happened in the back of the limo happen again.

Instead, she would tell Alex what she knew about Preston Wellington III. She regretted not telling him last night before the limo ride. But he'd asked for one night without any bad news. And she had to admit, she'd enjoyed herself immensely.

Meanwhile she had a wedding to take care of, then she would be flying to Tennessee to find out what she could about Presley Wells.

She was her usual quiet self as she loaded into the van with the rest of the Miami Confidential team.

The talk among the group was of everything but weddings—and undercover work. Samantha leaned against a side window and listened, enjoying the fact that today they were all women and could chat about the craziest things.

Fortunately, the road to Key Largo was open, the traffic not too bad. Samantha breathed a sigh of relief when they arrived and saw that all of the details she'd so meticulously been working on with the rest of the team seemed to be in place.

This was a part of her job that she loved. Often it rivaled the other part of her job. But surprisingly, she had become a pretty good wedding planner.

The beach and leased hall for the reception were beehives of activity. Samantha checked in with Nicole O'Shea, Weddings Your Way's photographer; Jeff Walsh, the shop's music coordinator; and finally Ethan Whitehawk, the team's all-around handyman. The three had ridden down together earlier. Ethan had been involved in building an arch on the beach where the actual wedding would take place.

"The arch is beautiful," she told him. "I've heard nothing but raves."

As was his nature, Ethan only smiled as he made some minor changes to the outdoor bandstand.

Samantha left him and saw that Isabelle, the shop's spokeswoman, was talking to the mother of the bride as if trying to reassure her. Samantha started over but Isabelle motioned that everything was fine.

Normally, this many agents didn't attend the weddings. Most of them worked behind the scenes before the big day and weren't needed.

But this was the first wedding since Sonya Botero had been abducted. Rachel had worried that what had happened wasn't an isolated incident. That instead, another bride-to-be from Weddings Your Way might be in danger, so the whole team had come.

Samantha opened her notebook and began to check off items to be attended to. Alex Graham was hardly in her thoughts as she did what she did so well: tended to details.

The team disappeared during the wedding, all breathing a collective sigh of relief that there had been no problems. The weather had held, all the guests had arrived and the ring bearer hadn't lost the rings. All small miracles.

And maybe a larger miracle. The bride-to-be had made it through her vows without any problems—including another abduction or hit-and-run.

Samantha had already made sure the reception hall was ready, fully decorated, the wedding cake in its place with the small plastic bride and groom snugly on top.

She started to retreat as the guests filed in. Behind them she caught a glimpse of the turquoise water and sunlight. She had only a moment to appreciate it before someone stepped into her line of vision.

"I wondered if you would be here," the man said.

He'd taken her by surprise. "Mr. Graham."

"Brian," he said, seeing her moment's hesitation. "Obviously I didn't make as big an impression on you as my brother."

There was an edge to his tone.

"I didn't realize we were on a first-name basis," she said.

"Even after I lent you my limo last night? I was surprised to see the two of you on what certainly appeared to be a date."

She ignored the last part. "Thank you for the use of your car. That was very generous of you," she said, hoping to get away from him as quickly as possible. Clearly he was curious about her relationship with Alex.

Brian resembled his brother only slightly. Unlike

Alex, Brian didn't look particularly fit. He was pale skinned as if the only light he spent much time under was fluorescent. His hair was a darker blond, his eyes brown but without any of the gold flecks that warmed Alex's.

The little time that she'd spent around Alex's brother and father had been sufficient to convince her Alex's problems with them weren't all his fault.

"You really *are* a wedding planner," Brian said, seeming to find amusement in that.

"Did you doubt it?" she asked.

He didn't answer, just studied her openly. She felt his gaze light on her bruised cheek but he said nothing about that. "I heard you do all the big weddings," he said instead.

So he'd been checking up on her.

"There must be money in it." He made it sound as if that would be the only reason someone would resort to her kind of work.

She wondered what he'd have to say if he knew about her other job. She smiled as patronizingly as she could, not about to answer such a crass question.

"So did you find my sister's fiancé?"

"Not yet."

"I'm sure my brother won't stop until he does," Brian Graham said. "I guess he doesn't have anything better to do."

Odd the way he didn't refer to his siblings by their names, not to mention his condescending tone.

"I'm sure when Alex finds Preston, he'll be glad your

brother went to the trouble. After all, we're talking about Preston's future wife," she said, not at all sure of that anymore, given the man's name wasn't even Preston.

"Has it dawned on you yet that maybe Pres doesn't want to be found?" Brian asked.

As a matter of fact… Out of the corner of her eye she spotted one of the caterers looking around frantically.

"If you'll excuse me, I need to attend to a few more details," she said.

"The perils of being a wedding planner," he said glibly as she left him.

But she felt his gaze on her, and later, when she finished calming down the caterer, she was surprised to see that Brian Graham was still standing where she'd left him, apparently watching her.

She turned away, hoping to avoid any more conversation with him, and almost collided with the black sheep of the Graham family.

"*Alex*," she cried, hating how breathless she sounded.

It surprised—and upset—her how pleased she was to see him.

That was until she caught his expression.

"Miss Peters," he said.

So they were back to that?

"I didn't know you were going to be here," she said.

He raised a brow. "Actually, I didn't, either."

There was something very different about him today. She saw it in his eyes. He seemed wary of her. Yesterday, she'd caught him watching her closely as if trying to see beneath her skin, today his gaze probed even deeper, definitely looking for something.

She felt a sliver of worry burrow under her skin. What had changed? Something more than even the phone call in the limo last night.

"How is Caroline?" she asked, afraid that was the cause.

He scrubbed a hand over his face. "They took her into surgery for her broken leg this morning but she is improving all the time." His gaze came back to hers and she saw the suspicion in his eyes.

It gave her a strange sense of loss that affected her more than she wanted to admit. He didn't trust her anymore and she felt sick at the thought.

Without his trust she couldn't do her job.

But she knew that wasn't what made her sick to her stomach. She liked Alex Graham. Was attracted to him. More than that, she had to admit. He was the first man in a long time with whom she'd actually let her guard down. She could have fallen in love with him. Had already started.

The thought shocked her and at the same time, admitting it made her feel a little more steady on her feet. It was one of the reasons he unnerved her.

"Anything wrong?" he asked.

She blinked at him. "Why would you ask that?"

"Because you're frowning at me," he said, his eyes intent on her face. He reached over before she could draw back and brushed his fingers over the bruise on her cheek. "How did you say you did that again?"

He seemed to be waiting for her to explain the bruise and anything else she had to hide. She gulped, not sure what he wanted from her. Worse, what she might confess. "Like I said, I can't even remember. I bumped into something obviously."

He seemed disappointed in her. "Obviously."

A strained silence fell between them. He raked a hand through his hair, his gaze on her. "Can we get out of here?"

She hated to think what would happen if she went off some place alone with him the way she was feeling right now. Fortunately, she didn't get a chance to answer.

Brian came up behind his brother. "So where is Preston?" he demanded, clearly enjoying that he'd interrupted their conversation. Samantha smelled booze on his breath. "You have found him, haven't you?"

Alex didn't look the least bit happy to see his brother. "What do you care?"

"She's my sister, too. But for some reason you seem to need to play the hero. So where is he?" Brian's eyebrows shot up. He smiled obnoxiously. "What? The great Alex Graham, brave fireman and all-around good-guy blue-collar worker, couldn't find him, either?"

Alex visibly tensed. "Back off, Brian. Today is not the day to cross me."

"Oh? Having a bad day?" Brian glanced at Samantha. "Things not going quite like you'd hoped?" He laughed. "Stick to what you know, Alex. Let me handle cleaning up the mess Caroline made."

"So you and Dad did invest with him," Alex said. "I hope you and the old man lose your shirts. I'd love to see this guy take you for everything."

Brian's face turned a mottled dark red. "Don't you think I know you're just waiting for me to fail? But don't hold your breath, little brother. I will come out on top. No matter what."

"I'm sure you will," Alex said. "But I'm not worried about you. Or Dad. Caroline is in love with this guy. If he really did hook up with her just to get to you and the old man, it's going to break her heart."

Brian scoffed. "Caroline will get over him. With her money, she can always find another man. Dad, however, stands to lose considerably. If I were you, I'd worry about your inheritance."

Samantha could see that Alex was doing everything in his power to restrain himself. "It's always about the money with you, isn't it? Have you ever been in love? Or lost someone who meant something to you?"

Brian's eyes sparked with fury. "Oh, none of us could have loved and lost with such feeling as you, Alex."

"I don't want to argue with you."

Brian hadn't seemed to hear him. "You have no idea what it takes to run an empire, the responsibility, the pressure. I don't have the luxury of whiling away my time falling in and out of love."

"No, your idea of love is the twenty minutes you pay for a woman's company."

Brian looked as if he might take a swing at his

brother. When he spoke, his words seemed to vibrate with his fury. "You know nothing about my life or how hard it is to be the one in the family who everyone depends on. You turned down the job. You couldn't handle it even if you hadn't. So stay the hell out of it." With that, he stormed away.

"What an arrogant ass," Alex said through gritted teeth.

Samantha touched his arm. He was trembling.

He looked over at her. "Please, let's get out of here." He didn't wait for an answer, just took her hand and drew her out the door.

"Alex, I—"

"I need to talk to you." There was a command in his tone. But also a plea.

She couldn't have denied him anything right then. "All right. Just let me tell someone I'm leaving."

He seemed to relax a little. "I know a place we can go. It's cool and dark. I don't know about you, but I could use a drink." He steered her toward his pickup.

The last thing she wanted was a cool, dark, intimate place to go with him, let alone a drink. Isn't that the way it had started last night?

He didn't drive far before he pulled into a small beach bar overlooking the water. As he shut off the engine, she heard music drifting on the warm afternoon breeze. The air smelled of sand and surf with the faint scent of burgers and fries and beer.

Once inside, he headed straight for the crowded bar. She hesitated by the door, half-afraid of what he wanted to talk to her about. Maybe it was just her guilty conscience, but she felt an icy chill skitter up her spine.

Then she glanced behind her and spotted a car parked just down the street. She couldn't be sure, but it looked like the one that had been following them before. It was hard to see if there was anyone behind the wheel because of the glare off the windshield. Had they been followed? Again?

She stepped back out of the bar and walked toward the car, turning down a short alley and circling around in order to come up behind it. The car looked like a rental. There was no one behind the wheel and on closer inspection she could see that the car was locked.

She glanced around but didn't see anyone who looked suspicious. Maybe the driver had gone into one of the businesses and was watching her.

She made a quick call to Clare to run the plates. "I think you're going to get a rental car agency. Find out who rented the car and let me know ASAP."

As she headed back inside the bar, she told herself she wouldn't be surprised if the car was rented by Presley Wells. It wouldn't be the first time she'd been dead wrong about a man. Or the last, she thought as she saw the expression on Alex's face.

He stood by the door to the beach with a drink in each hand, a frown on his face. "Let's take these outside."

She started to lie and tell him she'd been trying to find the ladies' room. But she was tired of lying to him and determined to end it here today.

He didn't say another word as he put down the drinks at one of the empty tables and pulled up a chair. He seemed to be waiting for her to say something.

She picked up the margarita he'd ordered her and touched her tongue to the salt, avoiding his gaze as she looked out over the water and thought about how to tell him the bad news.

ALEX HAD PLANNED to ask Samantha outright as soon as he saw her if she'd gone back to Caroline's condo the night after they'd been there together.

Looking at her now, though, the question seemed ludicrous. What possible motive would a wedding planner have to break into anyone's condo? It made no sense.

What did make sense was someone trying to make him distrust her. Trying to muddy the waters. He and Samantha had been working together to find Caroline's fiancé. Someone didn't like that. It told him that he and Samantha were getting close.

Even with all that wonderful rational thinking, Alex knew he was kidding himself. He'd already suspected that Samantha was hiding something from him. Now he would be watching her. And she already intrigued him.

"You look pretty today." He meant it. Even with the bruise on her cheekbone.

The compliment seemed to embarrass her. He watched her swallow and look away and a sinking feeling gripped his stomach. He still wanted to believe that the call last night had been a prank.

He raised his glass and said, "To you, thank you for all your help."

Samantha raised her plastic glass trying not to squirm. He couldn't have made her feel more guilty than if he'd toasted to honesty.

She didn't drink alcohol other than an occasional glass of wine. She liked to be in control. Always.

And, she needed all the control she could muster around Alex. The last thing she needed was alcohol and this beautiful beach on this wonderful afternoon. Her defenses were already down at just the hint of his smile.

"To happy endings," she said, wondering where that had come from, and took a sip, pleasantly surprised at how good it tasted.

She licked the salt from her lips, the alcohol in the margarita sending a shot of heat through her. She could feel Alex watching her, measuring her. The man definitely made her feel unsettled, unsure. Vulnerable. But it was the other emotions he made her feel that scared her. Especially the big one: desire.

She recalled the last time she'd felt desire—and how badly it had ended. She reminded herself that she was happy being a chameleon, blending in, going unnoticed by men.

She didn't want her life disrupted by him stirring up feelings, needs. She felt oddly exposed as if for all her care at hiding behind her glasses, her clothes, her front at Weddings Your Way, he could see through her.

It was the way he looked at her. There were moments

when she was positive he could see right through her veneer to her deepest, darkest of all secrets. Not only that she was an agent but that her real guise was pretending to be a wallflower so she didn't attract men like Alex Graham.

Was it possible Alex already knew that while she was cool and collected on the outside, she was a mess below the surface whenever she was around him? That it was a battle to keep anything from him?

Her heart beat a little faster at the thought that he knew her and that was one of the reasons she felt so drawn to him.

He started to say something but stopped as a waiter slid a basket and a dish with what looked like jalapeño peppers onto the table.

"Wait until you taste this." He stabbed one of the pepper slices with his fork, uncovered the warm bread, took a piece and shoved the pepper into it before he holding to her lips, his gaze meeting hers.

There was nothing she could do but open her lips, all of her senses on alert at the intimacy of him feeding her.

Hesitantly she took a bite. The bread was warm and wonderful, the pepper both hot and sweet. She'd never tasted anything like it.

"I knew you'd like it." He sounded a little sad, the pad of his thumb deliciously rough as he dabbed at the corner of her mouth when some of the pepper juice escaped. She felt the sudden intense heat of the pepper.

But it was nothing compared to what the look in his

eyes did to her. Heat skittered over her skin, firing her senses and sending a shaft of desire straight to the heart of her.

"Well?" he asked.

She took a drink and had to swallow twice before she trusted herself to speak. "Wonderful."

He smiled that beguiling smile of his. "That was just the beginning. There are more surprises in store."

She was almost positive he wasn't referring to food now.

He didn't want to ask her if she'd gone back to the condo last night. But he knew he couldn't put it off any longer.

He wiped his mouth on his napkin then took a drink of his margarita. Funny, but he hated to disappoint her. He knew how much she was hoping that Preston would turn out to be one of the good guys.

Putting down his glass, he said, "I'm afraid it's just as I feared. Caroline is broke. I have connections at the bank. She's gone through most of her inheritance. From what I can tell she's completely financing the condo development along with her own condo renovation. The checks are being run through Preston Wellington III's construction company." He could see that Samantha wasn't any happier to hear this than he had been.

She took a sip of her drink, lashes hiding her eyes, and said nothing, giving him the impression that, as bad as this news was, it hadn't exactly come as a surprise.

"You still want to believe in him, don't you?" he said.

"For Caroline's sake and the baby's? Yes, I do."

He sighed, unable to wait any longer. "I went to Caroline's condo last night after I got a call that someone had broken into it."

Something flashed in her eyes—or had he just imagined it?

"The champagne glasses and bottle were gone and the bathroom was shot up," he said. "There were two bullets in the wall where the bathroom mirror used to be." His gaze locked with hers.

He hadn't realized how much he was hoping she would say she didn't know anything about it. For the life of him, he couldn't think of a good reason she would break in to steal an empty champagne bottle and two dirty glasses.

Unless she was covering for somebody.

And he hoped to hell that wasn't the case, since he was falling for her.

She opened her mouth and said the last thing he wanted to hear. "I was the one who broke into the condo and took them."

Chapter Twelve

Alex let out a curse and rose, almost knocking over their drinks as he reached for her hand. "Come on."

He headed down the nearly deserted beach, practically dragging her. The sun hung low on the horizon, a ball of golden fire that cast the afternoon in dramatic light.

They hadn't gone far when she stopped to pull off her sensible heels. He let go of her hand and watched her slip off one shoe, then the other, her toes digging into the warm sand. Her toenails were painted a bright red. For some reason it made him smile—even as angry as he was.

He turned away from her and walked farther down the beach until he reached a small cove surrounded by water, rocks and trees. The place was secluded and they were completely alone.

She hadn't caught up to him yet. He watched her walk through the white sand, the turquoise water behind her, and couldn't help but remember the feel of her in the back of the limo last night. Looking at her, he would never guess that there were amazing curves beneath that boxy suit jacket. Or that the woman looking at him right now could be as passionate as the one he'd kissed last night.

He walked slowly back to her, never taking his eyes from her face. When he reached her, he cupped her cheek, thumbed away a tear, then rubbed the pad of his thumb over her full lips remembering how his mouth had felt on them, remembering the taste of her as he dragged her into his arms.

Her eyes widened, her lips parting. He heard her sharp intake of breath, felt the slight tremble in her body, as his mouth dropped to hers.

The moment their lips touched electricity arced between them setting off a storm in him. He felt a flash of desire as sharp and intense as a bolt of lightning. It set off a fire that rushed through his veins.

He grabbed the back of her suit jacket, fisting the material in his hands as he dragged her tighter against him until he could feel her wonderful body even through the fabric.

She quaked in his arms as his tongue explored her lips, her mouth, as if he could break through her cool reserve and unlock her secrets.

She wasn't so cool right now. Her mouth was hot and tasted of citrus and salt. He wanted nothing more than to go on kissing her forever.

He heard a chorus of giggles behind him and reluctantly withdrew his mouth to glance back and see a gaggle of young children all tittering, small hands over their mouths, eyes wide as platters. Behind them, several women who appeared to be day care providers gave him a disapproving look.

Alex could only smile as he opened his fists, released the wadded up fabric of Samantha's jacket and stepped back, but kept his arm around her. He could feel her still trembling, one of her arms around his waist, a piece of his shirt in her fist as though, if he let her go, her legs might not hold her up.

The interruption gave him time to come to his senses and he knew he should have been thankful for that. But he wasn't. His heart was beating wildly and desire still burned in every cell.

Who was he kidding? He wanted this woman even knowing what he did about her.

As ALEX STEPPED AWAY from her, Samantha sank down to the sand, not worrying about her expensive suit.

She was shaking, her head spinning, her body devoid of the strength to remain standing.

He looked down at her, a combination of anger and desire shining bright in his gaze. "Who are you?" he asked in a hoarse whisper. "Just when I think I know you…" Pain registered in his expression, a sharp anguish that squeezed her heart as if he held it in his fist.

He sank to his knees in front of her and took her shoulders again in his large hands.

All she could do was look up into his handsome face. The kiss had been so unexpected. He'd been angry at her, demanding answers. Why kiss her?

"Talk to me," he commanded. "Dammit, Samantha. Why would you break into Caroline's condo to steal an empty champagne bottle and two glasses?"

She tried to get to her feet, forcing him to rock back, giving her space but losing the smile, a hard wary edge to his expression.

She felt a little more in control again with distance between them although she was still shaking inside, her heartbeat slower but more painful. "I'm sorry I didn't tell you right away."

"Sure," he said, getting to his feet and turning his back to her, the Gulf of Mexico blue-green and endless.

Her eyes burned with tears as she stood and brushed sand from her suit. She wanted to step toward him, to place her hand on his back, to have him take her in his arms. She wanted him to make love to her.

The truth shocked her. She barely knew the man and yet she felt as if she knew him better than herself. Worse, he didn't know her.

Or maybe he did, she thought as she noted the angry set of his shoulders. She remembered the look on his face when she'd turned to see him back at the wedding reception.

She took a deep breath, smothering the urge to touch him and instead brushed again at the sand on her skirt, buying herself a little more time. Where was her famous cool now? And what was she going to do about these feelings?

"Alex…"

He glanced back at her. The look in his eyes hurt more than if he'd struck her. He didn't say a word. He didn't have to. She couldn't have denied him anything at that moment.

"Alex, I went back to Caroline's the other night. I took the champagne bottle and the glasses."

"Why would you do that?"

She was sick of lying but there were some things she couldn't tell him. She had to protect the anonymity of the team. She couldn't let what she was feeling for him cloud her judgment. Or worse, endanger their lives or those of the people involved in this case.

And yet she knew if she let him go on believing she'd betrayed his trust, she would never forgive herself. Alex Graham mattered. More than she ever dreamed a man could matter again. Every instinct told her not to trust her feelings. Not to trust another man. That it would end badly. That this time it would kill her.

"I took the bottle and glasses for fingerprints."

"What would a wedding planner need with fingerprints?"

Leave it to Alex to get straight to the heart of it.

"I have a friend who works at the lab." True enough.

"Why didn't you just tell me you wanted to take the champagne bottle and glasses when we were there together?" he asked. "I would have let you."

She swallowed. "I didn't know you well enough then." Which was laughable. She'd only known him a couple of days. And yet she believed she knew him now?

"I didn't want to upset you since I had no idea what I would find out."

He was shaking his head, his smile devoid of any humor. "Upset me? A call in the middle of the night telling me my sister's wedding planner is breaking into the condo upsets me. Lies upset me. Finding my sister's condo shot up upsets me." He reached out and brushed his fingertips lightly across her cheek.

She felt a stab of heat shoot straight to her center.

"Seeing that bruise on your cheek upsets me." He drew back his fingers. "What happened at the condo?"

"Someone showed up. He had a key—and a gun. I didn't get a look at his face."

Alex just stared at her. "You're telling me someone tried to kill you?"

She swallowed, holding his gaze, seeing the play of emotions cross his face and desperately wanting to tell him anything he wanted to know. "I managed to get away. Alex…" She started to reach for him, but he drew back.

"Who *are* you?" he asked again. His gaze cut to her core. "And what the hell is going on?"

SAMANTHA'S CELL PHONE rang. She flinched as if pained by the sound, reached into her bag and looked at the caller ID. "I'm sorry. I have to take this."

Alex let out a frustrated laugh. "Saved by the bell,"

he said, turning to walk a few yards up the beach, half-afraid of what he would do if he didn't put space between them.

He couldn't believe what an idiot he'd been. He didn't know what surprised him more—that she was admitting to breaking in to Caroline's condo or that she had a friend who could run fingerprints on champagne bottles and glasses.

At least she had told him the truth about being at the condo, although he wasn't fool enough to believe that's all there was to it.

Instead of demanding answers, he'd kissed her and only managed to make things worse. This wasn't about him. Or even about her, he reminded himself. It was about finding his sister's fiancé, finding out just how much trouble Caroline was in. And making sure she was okay.

He'd gotten sidetracked with this woman. He turned to look back at her. She was listening intently to whoever was on the other end of the line. The woman had more secrets than the CIA. Every instinct told him to give her a wide berth. The last thing he needed was another deceitful woman and he'd had his share.

He walked farther up the beach away from her, trying to get his head on straight. She'd broken into his sister's condo to get fingerprints. Amazing. And he thought the last woman who lied to him was bad. Hell, all she'd done was try to marry him for his money.

"Sorry, I had to take that," she said behind him.

He braced himself before he turned. She'd taken off her suit jacket. Her arms were lightly freckled, her skin much fairer than he'd realized.

She squinted up at him, one hand raised to shield her eyes. "I need to go back."

He nodded. "Wedding business, right?" He hadn't meant to sound so scornful. The sun was in her face and he saw now the sprinkling of tiny golden freckles across her nose and cheeks that she normally kept so well hidden under makeup. "What is your real hair color?"

"*What?*"

"That brown, it's not your natural hair color, is it?"

Her eyes widened a little. "I don't understand why—"

"Never mind," he said. "It doesn't matter. Like you said, you need to get back." He turned and started down the beach away from her.

"Red," she called after him.

He stopped walking but didn't turn around again.

"I'm betting it's a strawberry blonde." He heard a catch in her throat.

He turned slowly to look back at her. There were tears in her eyes.

"His name isn't Preston Wellington III," she said. "It's Presley Wells. He has a record, served time jail for burglary. He took out a large insurance policy on your sister, five million dollars. I'm going to his hometown in Tennessee to see if I can find him."

"And you are…?" he whispered.

Her eyes filled and he had the feeling that it took every once of her strength to keep the tears from spilling. "A wedding planner. Among other things."

He nodded. "And who called me last night and told me you were at Caroline's condo?"

She shook her head. "It had to be the man who shot at me. I'm fairly sure no one else saw me there."

He said nothing for a moment as he shifted his gaze from her to the water. "Wouldn't you say the chances were good that the man you had your little…run-in with at the condo was this Presley Wells?"

"I can't say. He was average height and weight—like half the men in Southern Florida."

"Except half the men in Southern Florida don't have a key to Caroline's condo," he said, looking at her again. "I'm going to Tennessee with you unless you have a problem with that."

"If that's what you want."

He studied her for a long moment. "Eventually, you're going to tell me what your investment is in all this, aren't you."

Her gaze softened. "Maybe."

He shook his head again. "I must be crazy." But at least this way he could keep an eye on her—for more reasons than he wanted to list. He just had to be careful and not get too close, although he had a bad feeling it was too late for that.

SAMANTHA WATCHED Alex on his cell phone as he made arrangements for a chartered flight to Tennessee this afternoon.

He didn't trust her. But who could blame him?

She hated this. But there was no way around it. She had a job to do. It didn't matter what Alex Graham thought of her. All that mattered was getting to the bottom of Sonya Botero's abduction. And while Samantha didn't want to believe Presley Wells was behind it any more than she believed he was behind Caroline's hit-and-run accident, she knew she had to go to Tennessee and find out the truth.

"So where do we fly into?" Alex asked.

Samantha told him the town Clare had given her. "Knoxville would be the closest airport. We'll have to drive down into the Smoky Mountains south of there."

Alex hesitated, then said into the phone, "I'll need a four-wheel drive rig waiting for us at the airport. That's right. Just as soon as we can fly out."

Two hours later, Samantha was sitting across from Alex in a soft leather seat, the rest of the small jet empty except for the pilot. She hated to think what this was costing Alex, but apparently he could afford it.

Samantha closed her eyes as the plane took off, recalling her hurried phone conversation with Rachel before takeoff. The Holcom-Anders wedding had gone off without any trouble. No more Weddings Your Way clients abducted or injured. But also no ransom demand on Sonya Botero yet.

"I'm on my way to Tennessee," Samantha told her. "Alex is chartering a plane."

"You told him then?" Rachel asked.

"I couldn't keep this from him."

"Have you blown your cover?"

"No."

"But you've considered telling him you're an agent." It wasn't a question. "I would think long and hard about doing that. You could be jeopardizing the team—let alone your own life. I don't think I have to remind you that in this business you have to be very careful who you trust."

"No, you don't have to remind me," Samantha said.

"Let me know as soon as possible what you find out in Tennessee." Samantha had heard the warning in her boss's voice and the disappointment. Samantha's cover had been blown only once before while in the FBI but she was sure Rachel knew about it. That time it had cost her dearly but she feared this time it could cost her her life.

"So who was he?" Alex asked.

Her eyes came open with a start. *"What?"*

"The man who let you down, who was he?"

She stared at him. Alex had to be a mind reader. "I don't know what—" She stopped. His gaze held so much compassion. She looked away. "What would make you think—"

"You don't have to tell me if you'd rather not," he said and turned to look out the window. Wisps of clouds blew past against a backdrop of blue. She caught a glimpse of the Gulf as the plane banked and headed for Tennessee.

"I met him after college," she said, her voice barely a whisper. Alex said nothing. He didn't look at her and for that she was grateful. "It was the first time I'd been serious about anyone. Even at the time, it seemed too good to be true. It was. He'd been playing me to get to my roommate—his real target."

He looked at her then, his gaze filled with empathy. "I'm sorry."

She nodded, deciding to tell him all of it. "The thing was, my roommate didn't want him. His obsession led to him kidnapping and killing her. He's on death row now."

Alex's eyes widened in shock. "My God."

She didn't tell him that she and her roommate were both FBI agents working undercover or that her cover was blown and her career almost lost before the man was captured.

"He totally fooled me," she said. "What does that say about me?"

He shook his head. "That you're trusting. His kind are pathological liars with no feelings other than basic survival instincts. It's like they were born with something missing inside them. They're so good at lying, no one can see through them." He fell silent. "I'm afraid this Presley Wells might be one of them, that's how he fooled my sister." He looked over at her. "You do realize that all men aren't like that, right?"

"It's just hard to trust your instincts after something like that," she said quietly. "I've always felt I should have seen what was going on. If I had, I might have been able to save Meredith."

He reached over and took her hand. "You certainly aren't the first woman to be taken in by a man. At least you weren't pregnant with his baby."

"My instincts told me that Preston...Presley was a good man," she said with a lift of her brow. "If I'm wrong about him, too..."

"Then you could be wrong about *me*?"

Heat warmed her cheeks. She looked away. "It's not quite the same thing."

"No," he said. "It's not, because I'm not like either of those men."

Silently she said the words she couldn't bring herself to voice. How time will tell.

VICTOR CONSTANTINE watched the plane until it disappeared into the clouds before he made the call. "They just left in a chartered plane for Knoxville, Tennessee." He held the phone away at the sound of loud swearing.

"I want them stopped. Whatever you have to do."

Victor frowned. "How would I stop them? Shoot down the plane?"

"Not *now*, you fool. Catch the next flight to Knoxville, Tennessee. Take care of them out there. The roads where they're headed are narrow mountain lanes. It should be easy for you to make sure they never make it back here."

"Do you realize what you're asking me to do?" Victor said mentally adding up the cost for two murders.

"I'm not *asking* you. I'm telling you. I want them taken care of."

"Then we'd better discuss my fee." He tossed out a number, having no desire to go to Tennessee. And even less desire to kill Samantha Peters. He'd missed catching her at home last night and clearly tonight was out, but maybe when she returned…

"I'll pay you double your fee. Just make sure that neither of them returns to Miami." The phone went dead.

His client had just raised the stakes. Only a fool would turn down that kind of money.

He waited, not surprised when his cell phone rang. "Yeah?"

"I've chartered you a jet. You're still at the airport, right?"

"Right."

"Take down this address in Tennessee. The area is isolated, nothing but squirrels, mountains and timber."

"You want it to look like an accident?"

"That would be nice but not necessary. I just want them both dead."

Chapter Thirteen

They hadn't talked the rest of the short flight. Samantha had dozed. Or possibly pretended to. It gave Alex a chance to just look at her. He had so many questions. At least one of the big ones had been answered.

He knew the first time he'd touched her that she was more than a little gun-shy when it came to the opposite sex. He knew the look, the feelings, the reactions. He'd been burned himself and hadn't even dated in months. It took a while to trust again and he wasn't to that stage yet himself.

But he couldn't imagine going through what she had. It proved how strong she was.

He wondered if that was why she'd changed her hair, tried to hide her body beneath the oversize suits. She came off as an ice princess when there was molten lava burning inside her. Their kisses had proven that.

She was scared of those feelings. So was he. And with good reason. She knew who he was. He couldn't say the same of her. More than a wedding planner. But how much more?

Once they landed, Samantha gave him directions and they left Knoxville and quickly found themselves in the Smoky Mountains.

As they left the city and the roads became steeper and narrower, he caught her several times watching her side mirror. With a jolt, he realized why. "You think we've been followed?"

"It wouldn't be the first time," she said. "Someone's been following us since the day Caroline was injured in the hit-and-run."

He gritted his teeth. "And you didn't bother to mention it?" How did she know about these things anyway?

She seemed to let that go without comment.

"Isn't it pretty obvious who would be following us?" he asked. "Let's see. Who lied about who he was? Who doesn't seem to want to be found?"

"It could be someone who's hoping we'll find Presley for them," she said.

He saw her expression. "Like my brother or my father?" He let out a curse. He hadn't thought of that.

The road was now only a single lane as it climbed up a series of switchbacks. "You sure we're on the right road?"

She was staring back at the road behind them. "It shouldn't be much farther according to the directions we got back at the station."

"Don't get me wrong, I wouldn't put it past either my

brother or my father to hire someone to follow us. But you can't think they hired the guy who almost killed you the night in the condo."

"I don't think he came there to kill me. Maybe scare me. But then I surprised him," she said.

He glanced over at her, recalling what had happened at the hospital when he'd sneaked up behind her. "I'm sure you did." He had to shift into four-wheel drive to make the next switchback up the mountain. "Or maybe he was there for the same thing you were. Maybe he'd realized he'd left something incriminating in the condo and had gone back to retrieve it. I'm putting my money on Presley Wells. Unless you know something else I don't."

"I don't know any more than you do now."

He shot her a look, wanting to believe her. Up ahead, the road flattened out a little and he spotted an old rusted mailbox with WELLS printed in crude letters on the side. "Looks like we found it."

As SAMANTHA CAUGHT a glimpse of the house set back in the woods, she felt her stomach knot. The house had once been white but was now in desperate need of paint. Wash flapped on the clothesline out back and trash burned in a fifty-five-gallon barrel off to the side, the smoke rising slowly to fill the air with a rank smell.

Alex brought the rental SUV to a stop in the rutted yard sending a half-dozen chickens scurrying across the bare dusty ground. Several old dogs slept in the shade, not even stirring as flies swarmed around them. Through

the tall weeds along the side of the house she could make
out the remains of aging vehicles rusting in the sun.

"You all right?" Alex asked as he parked next to a
battered old pickup.

She could only stare at the house. She knew this kind
of poverty, this kind of despair. She'd lived it in Iowa,
where she'd grown up, and had run like hell from it the
first chance she got.

"Samantha?"

She nodded, not trusting her voice, as she caught
movement behind the faded curtains. Faded like her
mother after having so many children and being caught
in a cycle of hopelessness.

"You don't have to come with me if you don't want
to," Alex said, obviously seeing her hesitation to get out
of the car.

She could feel his gaze on her, that same curious
searching look he'd been giving her for several days
now. How much could he see? Could he see her fear at
the possibility of witnessing her earlier life in this
family's faces? Did he have any idea what a coward she
was when it came to her past?

She'd been running all her life, she thought as she
opened her car door in answer and got out. A rusted
sprinkler spat out a trickle of water in a tight circle near
the porch on what might have once been a lawn but was
now a mud hole. The sun was an oppressive ball of heat
directly overhead. It beat down on her as she walked
toward the rotting porch steps, Alex by her side.

The porch sat at a slant, the boards weathered and rotted. The smell from the trash hit her again and Samantha was struck with the image of her mother, her body thin and stooped, wearing a worn old housedress and slippers, taking out the trash to be burned.

The woman who opened the door could have been Samantha's mother. She wore a worn-thin homemade housedress, her graying hair limp and hanging around her narrow weary face.

"Yes?" she asked, squinting into the bright day as she eyed first Alex, then Samantha.

"Mrs. Wells?" Alex asked.

"Yes?" She looked at them suspiciously as if they were bill collectors.

Alex seemed at a loss as to what to say to the woman and glanced at Samantha. "I know your son Presley," she said.

The woman raised a brow, her narrowed eyes filled with even more suspicion. "He done something?"

"No, it's nothing like that," Samantha assured her. "His fiancé has been in an accident and we're just trying to find him to let him know." Her voice sounded shaky but not half as unsteady as she felt.

The woman looked more than skeptical and Samantha realized it was the kind of story that bill collectors used to come up with when they were trying to track down her daddy.

"I'm Samantha Peters," she said, holding out her hand to the woman.

Mrs. Wells ignored it.

"I'm planning Caroline and Presley's wedding and this is her brother Alex Graham," Samantha continued, dropping her trembling hand to her side again, feeling the dampness. She wiped her palm on her skirt trying to find that cool she'd once been so famous for. It had deserted her.

The woman frowned. "Caroline? That the woman he goin' to marry?"

"Could we step inside?" Alex asked, swatting at the flies swarming around them.

With obvious reluctance the woman stepped back. "But I ain't got no idea where he is."

Samantha stepped into the living room. Even the smells took her back to her childhood. The house was unbearably hot and dank. Everything looked as worn-out as Presley's mother.

"He don't come here no more," she said, wiping her hands on her dress. "Ya'll want to sit down. I got some sweet tea—"

Samantha glanced toward the sagging couch and felt Alex's gaze on her. "Are you all right?" he whispered.

She felt light-headed but nodded. "Fine."

"Thank you, but we can't stay," he said to Mrs. Wells.

"Did Presley tell you anything about Caroline?" Samantha asked.

She shrugged. It seemed to take all her energy. "He mighta said somethin' in his last letter."

"Do you remember the letter's postmark? Where it was mailed from?" he asked.

"Miami. He lives down there," she said. "You sure he ain't in trouble with the law again?"

"Why would you ask that?" Alex said.

The woman made a face. "His letters. There's money in 'em." She looked up at Samantha. "Says he's an... investor. Don't know what that is but it don't sound legal."

Samantha saw Alex hide a grin.

"Investing can be legal," Samantha said.

The woman didn't look as if she believed that.

Samantha pulled one of her business cards from her purse. "If you hear from Presley would you let me know?"

Mrs. Wells took the card in her rough hands. Through the window Samantha could see the old-fashioned wringer washing machine out back. She remembered her mother bent over one.

"You should buy yourself an electric washing machine with some of the money Presley sends you," she said.

Mrs. Wells narrowed her eyes. "The one I got works good enough."

Samantha said nothing as four children, ages from about ten through sixteen, came running in through the back door. They all looked a little like the man who'd been with Caroline the first time the two had come in to talk about their wedding.

"How many children do you have?" Samantha asked, her voice cracking, and quickly softened the question by adding, "I come from a large family myself."

"Twelve, only six left at home."

Samantha nodded. Her own mother had her first child at fourteen and spent the next thirty years having babies. She could feel Alex's eyes on her, feel his surprise at hearing about her large family.

"Your husband gone?" Samantha asked, knowing he probably was, since there were no diapers on the clothesline.

"Died some years back."

A silence fell over the house.

"I always wished I'd grown up in a large family," Alex said into that silence.

Samantha looked away, not wanting him to see her contemptuous expression. He had no idea what it was like. But then he'd never been dirt-poor. Samantha had. So had Presley.

He is no different from you.

She cringed at the thought. It was true, though. Like Samantha, Presley had escaped what her father used to call the snake pit. But did anyone ever really escape the scars of their childhoods?

She thought about Presley sending money home in his letters but realized even crooks often still cared about their mothers.

"Thank you for your time," Samantha said. "We can see ourselves out."

Mrs. Wells said nothing as Alex opened the screen door and they stepped out on the porch.

As they crossed the porch, Samantha saw a face staring out at her from the trees and froze.

The girl stood watching them. She couldn't have been more than twelve. Her feet were bare, her dress too small and scrubbed as threadbare as the white sheets hanging on the clothesline, her hair straight as a stick hanging in dirty hanks on each side of her narrow face.

But it was the eyes that grabbed Samantha. She recognized that look because she had been that girl.

Maybe still was that girl inside.

As Samantha started down the stairs she was unable to take her eyes off the girl. That's why she didn't even realize she'd missed a step until she went sprawling forward. She saw Alex reach for her but he was two steps behind and she was falling too fast. She tried to catch herself, but her hand landed in the muddy yard and she fell to her knees.

Alex was there at once, helping her up. "Are you all right?"

All she could do was nod. Her hands were muddy and her clothing soiled. She looked at the spot where she'd seen the girl. She was gone. If she'd ever been there to begin with.

Tears burned Samantha's eyes.

"You *are* hurt."

Samantha shook her head harder, the tears impossible to stem. She'd thought she'd dealt with her past. She'd thought she'd escaped that life, that girl she'd been. But all the pain came gushing out, hot tears scalding her cheeks.

She pulled free of Alex and stumbled toward the rental car, trying to brush the mud from her hands and forearms, the dirt from her clothing. She heard Alex behind her. He handed her one of the raglike towels that had been hanging on the clothesline and opened the car door for her.

She wiped what she could from her with the towel, returned it to the clothesline even though it was now soiled and stumbled into the car seat, knowing how foolish she must look to him. It wasn't until he joined her in the car that she finally got the sobs to stop.

Alex started the engine and drove away from the house without a word.

Samantha didn't look back. Couldn't. She was afraid she would see the girl watching them, longing to go with them.

"I'm sorry."

He looked over at her, aghast. "What do you have to be sorry about?"

"For…for falling apart on you like that." She took a ragged breath. "I…I…"

"You don't have to explain," he said, glancing at her again as he drove.

ALEX WAS MENTALLY kicking himself for bringing her to Tennessee, to this place. He'd seen her reaction back there before she fell, before she broke down. Damn. He wanted to stop the car and pull her into his arms. But he feared that would be the worst thing he could do right now.

"That was me."

She'd spoken so softly he wasn't sure he'd heard her correctly.

"You?"

"That was my childhood back there," she said.

She couldn't be serious. But then he looked over at her and finally understood. "You're the Presley in your family, aren't you?"

She nodded and turned her face away.

"I shouldn't have brought you here. I'm sorry."

She shook her head. "I thought I'd gotten over my childhood, the poverty, the bleakness of that life, but seeing Mrs. Wells and her children…" She brushed a hand over her cheek, her eyes red and shiny from her tears.

Alex said nothing as he drove and tried to imagine what it would be like growing up back at that house.

SHE WATCHED THE TREES rush past, feeling foolish. She'd worked so hard to hide who she was from Alex and to break down like that…

Alex reached across, took her hand and squeezed it. "You must think I'm a real jackass complaining about my family."

Her throat hurt from trying not to cry again. "I've never thought you were a jackass."

He smiled then, those wonderful eyes of his brightening as he glanced at her. "You're just letting me off easy and we both know it." His gaze caressed her face. "You are one remarkable woman, you know that?"

She felt anything but remarkable right now.

He turned back to his driving and she watched the thick dark leaves of the trees brush over the SUV and thought about Presley Wells. Where was he? She couldn't shake the feeling that his mother was right and that not only was Presley in trouble, but so was Caroline.

"I don't want to be wrong about Presley," she said.

He looked over at her. "I don't want you to be wrong, either. You never suspected where he'd come from when you met him?"

"Just like you never suspected when you met me."

He smiled sheepishly. "No. But you made something out of yourself."

"Maybe Presley did, too."

"You didn't change your name."

"No," she admitted. "But I changed everything else." And yet she was still that poor, scared little girl inside.

Samantha saw a flash as something shiny caught in the sun on the side of the mountain ahead.

The back window of the SUV exploded. An instant later, the windshield turned into a spiderweb of white.

Chapter Fourteen

"What the—" Alex hit the brakes, at first not sure what was going on. The SUV went into a skid on the narrow road. He brought it back under control as his side window exploded.

"Keep your head down," he yelled as he hurriedly knocked out the windshield so he could see where he was going. The glass slid down the hood. He heard it crunch under the tires and cranked the wheel to make the next turn, almost too late.

Then he looked over at Samantha and saw what she had in her hand. A gun. He knew he shouldn't have been surprised. Hell, hadn't it crossed his mind that she had one in her purse back when he thought she was nothing more than a wedding planner? Nor did it seem he had to tell her someone was shooting at them.

"There!" she cried and pointed to a road that dropped almost straight off the mountain through a thicket of trees, the branches a canopy over the top. "Take it!"

"Hang on!" He jerked the wheel. The front tires dropped over the side and he felt as if he was hanging by his seat belt as the SUV careened downward through the trees. He tried to brake but the back tires hadn't touched down yet. He swore again as he sideswiped a stand of young maples, the saplings snapping off like toothpicks.

The back tires finally hit dirt and he was able to brake and shift down. Limbs scraped the top of the roof. They were still moving way too fast. And to make matters worse, he couldn't see what lay ahead. Could easily be a cliff or a ditch or a huge tree that would stop them dead.

He fought to get the rig slowed down and finally came to a halt in the heart of the thicket. They were completely closed in by the trees. They couldn't have opened their doors on either side and the SUV was sitting at such an angle, nose down, that he was practically standing on the brake pedal.

"You aren't hit, are you?" he was finally able to ask as he looked over at her, a tremor in his voice.

"I'm fine. Are you…?" She looked frightened at the thought.

"I'm just great," he said sarcastically. He'd really had it with this woman and her secrets.

She was looking back up the mountainside, the gun clutched in both hands in a way that convinced him it wasn't her first time. "I think we're far enough down the road he won't be able to take any potshots at us anyway."

"Wanna keep defending Presley Wells?" he asked her. "Unless there's someone else who wants to kill you for reasons you haven't told me."

"Not that I know of," she said.

"Let's try this again," he said, anger filling the hole fear had just deserted. "Who are you? What the hell is going on? And wait, how did you get that gun on the plane?"

She met his gaze, cool and calm, making him want to shake her. "Which question would you like answered first? As for what's going on, someone just tried to kill us."

"Okay, that part was pretty clear." He saw her glance back again. "You think he'll come down here and try to finish us off?"

"I think we'd better see where this road comes out since it doesn't look like turning around is an option," she said.

He didn't move, just glared at her, waiting. He wanted answers and he wasn't moving another inch until he had them. She'd put him off too long. His whole body was vibrating, adrenaline spiking his pulse as though he'd taken a wild drug.

She turned in her seat, her gaze locking with his. "I'm an agent."

He blinked. "An agent. Like—"

"Like FBI."

He pulled back in surprise. "I thought you were a wedding planner."

"I am. I'm both. I work undercover."

Yeah, right.

"You wanted the truth."

He did. But could he handle it? "You do this for a *living?*" An agent? The buddy at the crime lab, the wealth of information her "friends" came up with. He should have known. He shook his head. "I knew there was more to you, but I never guessed this. So you're after Presley Wells?"

"I'm *after* whoever abducted one of our wedding clients and ran down your sister. I'm still not sure who that is. But…" she added before he could argue, "I'm no longer convinced that your sister's fiancé is the man I thought he was."

"Well, I suppose that is something."

"Now could we get out of here?" she asked.

He studied her a moment longer. "You are definitely somethin'."

SAMANTHA WASN'T SURE he meant it as a compliment. In fact, she was pretty sure he intended it as just the opposite as he put the SUV into drive and let his foot up off the brake.

The car bounced down the mountain through the trees, Alex expertly handling it. She watched him, so filled with pain it took everything she could muster not to cry.

He was all right. He hadn't been hit by the gunfire. She tried to assure herself that he was safe. That after this she would make sure he stayed that way. Some agent she was. She'd almost gotten them both killed.

"Any idea which way to go?" he asked when he reached a fork in the steep road.

She had no idea but pointed to the left, her throat too dry to speak.

He reached over and cupped her cheek with his warm palm. "You didn't get me into this, so stop looking at me like it's your fault, okay?" He let up on the clutch and the SUV lurched downward again. "Damn this mountain is steep. But I got to hand it to you. Dropping off through here seems to have worked."

Ahead, through the trees, she saw a shallow creek where the road flattened out and another intersected it. Alex saw it, too. He drove across the shallow creek and turned on the more traveled road, looking over at her and grinning.

"What?" she had to ask.

"We're alive and, damn, but it feels good."

He made her smile, too, as he pulled her over, looping his arm around her, holding her close as he drove. When they hit the highway, he turned on the radio. He couldn't go fast, not with the missing windshield. He had to turn the radio all the way up. The wind whistled through the SUV, blowing back her hair.

She snuggled against him to the sound of country music. He was right. It felt damned good to be alive. Even better to be with Alex Graham.

At the first town, he pulled under the awning of a motel office just as it began to rain. The sky was dark, the clouds ominous. The radio announcer broke into the song to say that tornadoes had been seen and a weather alert was in effect. Just as Samantha feared, all flights had been canceled until further notice.

"I'll get us a room," he said, hopping out.

She caught sight of her reflection in the side mirror. Her hair was windblown, her face dirty and her clothing covered with dried mud. She looked as if she'd been in a pig wrestling contest and the pig had won.

He came back out with two keys and squatted next to her missing side window. He handed her the key to number nine, then seemed to see the tiny cuts on her face where the window had splintered and cut her. There were specks of dried blood mixed with dirt.

He swore. "Oh man, I didn't realize—"

"I'm fine," she said, taking his hand as he reached out to touch her cheek and kissing the palm. "I just need a bath. I'll be good as new." He didn't look convinced, but he opened her door and stepped back. "I'm next door if you need me." She had her purse, the weapon inside. She needed him, but not to protect her. At least not at the moment.

Inside the motel, she called Rachel and reported what had happened.

"You're sure you and Alex Graham are all right?"

"Yes." She fingered one of the cuts as she stared in the bathroom mirror. "There is no reason to report it to the locals. Whoever took the potshots at us is long gone." At least she hoped that was true.

"It had to be someone who knew where you were

going. Either Presley Wells or a member of his family," Rachel said.

It certainly looked that way. The shooter had positioned himself on the hillside using a high-powered rifle at a spot where he knew they would be most vulnerable.

"I think it is time to pick up Presley Wells for questioning," Rachel said and seemed to wait, expecting an argument. "If he's in the States, we'll find him."

Samantha doubted that. She had a feeling Presley was in hiding. But why, if he wasn't guilty as sin? "I'll get back to Miami as soon as I can. The weather…" It was tornado season. A hurricane whose name she couldn't remember had just come ashore in the redneck Riviera. This whole part of the country was expected to be drowning in water by midnight. Already she could hear the wind howling outside. All aircraft were grounded until further notice, according to the reporter on the radio.

"There is no rush," Rachel said. "Get some rest."

Samantha hung up and turned on the water in the shower. Then she stripped down, stepped under the wonderfully hot spray, and closed her eyes and thought about what could have happened on that mountain. The tears came then, tears of fear and relief, not for herself but Alex.

She quit crying, chastising herself for her moment of weakness—not her first today. As she shampooed her hair, she tried to drown out the sound of the SUV's windows exploding, the sound of the wind just outside, the eerie sound of silence around the Wells home and the vision of a young girl standing in the trees.

Samantha lathered soap over her body as if she could wash away the memories. It hadn't been just growing up poor. It was growing up without hope. When you were that poor, when you knew nothing but hardship, you didn't know there was a way out.

She thought of her family. Like Presley, she'd run away, trying to run fast enough to escape what had felt like quicksand pulling her down.

It was hard to explain to a man like Alex Graham who had grown up in his kind of wealth.

She didn't know how long she stood under the spray, letting the water pelt her skin until she was numb. Finally she shut off the water and stood for a moment in the tub listening to the wind and rain pelting the backside of the motel.

Presley was in trouble. That much she knew and would have bet the ranch on it. But was it of his making? It didn't matter now. The police would be on the lookout for him. What worried her was Caroline and the fear that Caroline might somehow be involved.

She dried with one of the large towels and wrapped her hair in another one turban-style, then pushed open the door, needing to let some of the steam out.

Her mind was working again, trying to fit the pieces together. It always came out the same. One big piece was missing. The centerpiece, the one that would give her all the answers. And that piece was Presley Wells.

She started to reach for her soiled clothing and

realized it was gone. For one startled moment, she thought her purse and gun were also missing.

But her purse was right where she'd left it on the counter within reach. Hurriedly, she checked. Her gun was still there. Still loaded. But her clothing was gone.

She peered into the bedroom and spotted a large shopping bag. Wrapping the towel more securely around her, she padded into the bedroom.

There was no one in the room but for the first time she noticed the adjoining room door. She'd bet the adjoining room was Number Eight—Alex's room.

Upending the bag, she dumped the clothing on the bed and gingerly picked up a pair of panties, surprised that he'd gotten the right size. He'd underestimated a little on the bra, but the top and skirt would fit perfectly. Too perfectly. How had he known?

The fabric was cut to slide over her curves. Even before she took the clothing back into the bathroom and put each item on, she knew there was no more hiding from him. She'd told him she was an agent, something she'd failed to tell Rachel, she realized.

She'd been so tired and dirty… No, she knew she'd purposely left that part out. She'd deal with it once she got back to Miami.

She looked at herself in the mirror, dragged the towel from her hair and tossed it aside. Finger-combing her hair, she watched it curl.

Alex had guessed that muddy brown wasn't her natural color. But wouldn't he be surprised to find out that she had naturally curly hair that she usually spent hours brushing straight each morning? She could see some of the red highlights in her hair. She'd had to skip her appointment to have the color covered this week because of what had happened at Weddings Your Way.

She stared at herself in the mirror, seeing her old self and wanting to flee from it. But at the same time, wanting to embrace it for the first time in years. This was all Alex's fault, she thought. He'd done this to her.

Behind her, there was a soft tap at the door. Anxiously, she raked her fingers through her hair again. But it was useless. Her hair was going to do what it wanted and that was curl.

Another tap.

She took a breath that sounded a lot like a sob.

Alex Graham was about to see the real her.

Her feet felt like lead weights, her legs rubber, as she walked to the door. With trembling fingers, she turned the knob, bracing herself for his reaction.

He let out a sharp breath, eyes widening. "Wow."

She felt self-conscious, just as she had as a young girl when her breasts had budded out early. She'd always been thin and having breasts had made her stand out. She'd hated the attention from the boys and did everything she could to hide her curves even back then. Now, though, she had no choice but to reveal her true self.

ALEX COULDN'T BELIEVE IT. Finally, he felt as if he was seeing the real Samantha Peters. "You look *fantastic*," he said. Tears welled in those big brown eyes of hers but she smiled, then worried at her lower lip with her teeth.

Without makeup, there was that adorable trail of tiny golden freckles that arched across the top of her high cheekbones over her perfect nose to the other cheek.

"Samantha." The word caught in his throat as his eyes met hers. Heat shot through him.

He had a flash of memory. His mouth on hers. The taste of her in the back of the limo. On the beach. He knew he was lost long before she stepped to him and, standing on tiptoe, gently touched her lips to his.

He didn't move. Didn't breathe.

She pulled back just enough to look into his eyes. Desire burned in her gaze but so did uncertainty.

She kissed him again, this time parting her lips to touch the tip of her tongue to his. Desire rocketed through him, as hot and moist as her mouth on his.

His arms came around her. He dragged her to him with a sound like a curse or an oath. Or a prayer. His hands splayed across her strong back as he dragged her even closer and kissed her as if there was no tomorrow.

He knew better than to get involved with another woman with secrets. But he could no more stop kissing her than he could forget the way she'd looked when she'd opened the door.

Heat blazed through his veins. Every instinct told him to stop as he cupped her wonderful behind in his hands and pulled her tightly against him.

She let out a gasp against his mouth but her arms had

found their way around his neck. She drew his lips down to hers again, her eyes sexy slits, as he lifted her and, kicking the motel room door closed, shoved her back against the wall.

He slipped her out of the slacks and slid his hand beneath the panties. She arched against him as his wet fingers took her to pleasure. Her own fingers found the buttons on his jeans and in moments he was driving into her. She cried out, her fingers twined in his hair. His mouth on one breast. He felt her release, a dam breaking. She slumped against him.

He wrapped her in his arms and carried her to the bed where he slowly made love to her again as the wind howled at the window and rain beat down in a steady torrent.

VICTOR CONSTANTINE made the call right after he saw the SUV careen over the side of the mountain and disappear into the trees. No one could have survived that.

He'd hoped for an explosion. Or at least to see flames. But he was convinced, even if they hadn't died at once, they would be injured too badly to ever climb back up that mountain to the road.

"That nasty little problem you had is taken care of," he said when his client answered. Victor had mixed feelings about it. He still wished he could have spent some quality time with Samantha Peters. He'd just have to find another woman like her and relieve this itch he had before he started his retirement.

"Good. Don't call again. As far as I'm concerned you and I never did business." The phone went dead.

Victor sat for a moment before he dialed his foreign bank. He couldn't put his finger on what was bothering him. Not until the bank representative took his password and told him his greatest fear had been realized. The client had wired money from an account which was then cleaned out and closed.

Another first for Victor Constantine. He'd been duped by a client. His last client.

He called the cell phone number the client had given him and wasn't surprised to get nothing. Not even a ring. No doubt the client had destroyed the phone, believing it was the only connection between them.

Victor smiled to himself, more amused than angry. Did the fool really think Victor Constantine would just let this go? Was anyone that stupid?

Apparently his former client was.

Victor couldn't wait until he found him, until he looked the man in the eyes and saw not just fear—but the realization that he was about to die a very painful death.

Chapter Fifteen

The phone woke Samantha from the most peaceful, contented sleep she could ever remember.

"Peters," she said, after groping her cell out of her purse beside the bed and snapping it open.

She could see a sliver of gray daylight coming through the blinds. It took her a moment to remember where she was. Last night came back in a rush. Her skin warmed at the memory and she swung her legs over the side of the bed and headed for the bathroom with a glance over her shoulder at Alex.

He lay on his side, eyes closed, an indentation in the bed where she had been snuggled next to him.

A feeling of euphoria flooded her. Had she ever been this happy? She found herself smiling as she closed the bathroom door.

"Samantha, can you hear me?" It was Rachel. She sounded worried.

"Yes. Sorry. I dropped the phone." She had tucked the

phone against her hip as she was looking back at Alex and now realized that Rachel had been speaking that whole time.

"Is everything all right there?" Rachel asked.

"Great." The word was out before she could catch it back. But it was the right one—just not one Rachel was used to hearing from her. "Fine. Everything is fine."

"I woke you," Rachel said.

Samantha glanced at her watch and realized it was after nine. "No, that is…" She mugged a face at the bathroom mirror, grimacing at how ridiculous she must sound. Rachel was no fool. Of course she could tell she'd awakened her.

"Is Alex there?"

"No." Samantha took a breath and let it out slowly. "He's in the next room."

"I see."

She figured Rachel did see.

"Does he know?"

Samantha didn't have to ask what she meant. "I had to tell him about me, but not about the team."

Silence, then, "You do understand that this puts your position in jeopardy?"

Samantha knew what she was asking. Was her relationship with Alex important enough to put her work on the line—as well as her life? "Yes."

"You surprise me, Samantha," Rachel said. "In the four years we've worked together has there been anyone else?"

"No. No one."

"And within a matter of days you have fallen for this man." It wasn't a question but Samantha answered it anyway.

"Yes. But it won't affect how I complete this assignment."

Rachel chuckled softly. "That's what they all say."

Samantha had seen others come and go at Miami Confidential. Some not under the best of circumstances. At least one had gotten herself killed. Samantha knew Rachel was concerned for her welfare—and that of their clients.

"I will do my job. No matter what," Samantha said with more force than she'd intended.

She could hear the smile in Rachel's voice when she spoke, "I believe that. Clare wants to talk to you. Let me know when you fly out."

"I will."

Clare came on the line. "I did that financial you asked for on both Presley Wells and Caroline Graham."

Samantha held her breath.

"Looks like they have everything invested in an area called Sunrise Estates."

The project where Caroline's condo was located. "So everything is riding on it?"

"Everything."

Samantha glanced toward the bathroom door. "I need you to check out a couple more names," she said and turned on the shower, covering her words. "Brian Graham, C. B. Graham and—" she took a breath and let it out slowly "—Alex Graham."

"What exactly am I looking for?"

"Any irregularities, recent large investments, anything that sends up a red flag," Samantha said. Rachel didn't think she could be impartial, objective. Rachel was wrong.

"I'll get back to you."

Samantha stepped into the shower feeling guilty and yet righteous. She had a job to do. If Alex was the man she believed him to be, he would understand that. She just prayed he *was* that man and that she hadn't just jeopardized not only her career but her life for a man she couldn't trust.

ALEX ROLLED OVER on his back and stared up at the ceiling. After a moment he heard the shower running and thought about joining Samantha.

Last night had been amazing. The intimacy they'd shared surprised him. He'd never felt anything like it before.

He heard the shower shut off. As he turned to watch her come out of the bathroom, one towel wrapped around her hair, the other around her slim body, he reminded himself who she was.

A federal agent masquerading as a wedding planner. He corrected that, a wedding planner masquerading as an ordinary woman.

Samantha Peters was no ordinary woman. Not by a long shot. And Alex Graham wondered if he could handle this much woman.

She stopped beside the bed and looked down at him. He wondered who'd been on the phone, but he only wondered if for a moment.

Light shimmered in her brown gaze like an expensive whiskey. He could smell the fresh scent of soap on her smooth skin. Her lips parted slightly and she knelt forward and kissed his cheek.

He closed his eyes, weak with desire for this woman. He opened them when he heard her straighten.

Slowly she took the towel from her head, dropping it on the floor. She raked a hand through her wet curly hair. She couldn't have been more beautiful, her skin glowing from the shower, her face flushed—just as it had been during their lovemaking.

And those eyes, deep and dark. His gaze locked with hers and a bolt of desire ricocheted through him, but he didn't move, barely breathed as he watched her.

Slowly, she unhooked the end of the towel wrapped around her. It dropped to the floor with barely a whisper.

She smiled at his intake of breath and was already leaning toward him as he threw back the covers and pulled her down on top of him.

THE STORM PASSED, leaving devastation in its wake. Everywhere there were downed trees and power lines. Once the hurricane farther south had come ashore it spawned high winds and tornadoes. One tornado had touched down not far from where they were staying.

As Alex drove them to the airport in the new rental

car he'd procured, they passed some of the debris. Samantha found herself wishing they didn't have to go back to their real lives.

And that surprised her. Her two jobs had been everything for so long, she'd never believed anything else could fulfill her the way her work did.

But that was before she'd met Alex Graham.

He'd grown quiet, as well. For a while they'd escaped everything, but those many hours together couldn't last and they both knew it.

Eventually, they'd known they would have to return to Miami. Samantha feared that would change everything. In Tennessee in a motel with Alex, she hadn't been a wedding planner or a special agent. She'd just been a woman.

ALEX HAD CALLED Caroline the minute the plane landed in Miami. His sister was doing much better. He hadn't talked to her that often over the years, so when she came on the line, he didn't really know what to say to her.

"Pres called," she said. "He feels so badly that he is out of the country and unable to return but he'll be home soon."

Alex knew she was lying, but he said, "Good. That must be a relief to you. I know about the baby, Caroline." Silence. "Hell, I'm ready to go out and buy a football. Or some dolls. It doesn't matter. I can't wait to be an uncle." He heard her crying.

"That's all I've ever wanted, Alex. For us to be a

family. You're going to love Pres. I planned to tell you about him the other day at Weddings Your Way…before the accident. I was just afraid you wouldn't understand. You know, about the baby and all."

"You know I'd love to talk to this fiancé of yours," Alex said. "Congratulate him and welcome him to the family. You have a number for him?"

Silence. Then, "He said the phones are terrible where he is, can't get calls in but he'll be calling me again soon and I'll tell him. He'll be glad and it won't be that long before you'll get to meet him in person."

Yeah right. "What country did you say he was in?"

More silence, then a weak laugh. "You know I didn't even ask. Somewhere in South America, I think he said. He moves around so much, who can keep track?"

It broke his heart to hear his sister try to cover for the man. How long did she think she could keep this up?

"Okay, sis," he said. "You just take care of yourself. I'll see you real soon." He had ended the call, anxious to get back to Miami, afraid for his sister even with an added guard on her room.

He understood that she'd lied about Pres because she loved the man. He understood love, maybe now more than he ever had before, he thought, looking over at Samantha as they walked through their terminal at Miami International Airport.

"Caroline says she's heard from Pres." He raked a hand through his hair. "I can hear the love in her voice for this guy. It kills me." He saw her expression. "I know you still want to believe in this guy, but if you're wrong about him, it doesn't mean you're wrong about me."

SAMANTHA HOPED that was true as she smiled and took his hand in hers. "I still believe he loves her." She couldn't have been wrong about that.

She wanted Presley to be innocent of any wrongdoing even more now that she'd met his family. She wanted him to be like her—the one who'd escaped that life, made good, prove it could be done. She needed that reassurance.

"If what you say about your father is true, he would never have accepted Caroline marrying Presley Wells of Tennessee," she said, trying to convince herself as much as Alex that that was the reason Presley had called himself Preston Wellington III.

Alex nodded slowly. "You saw how much my father admired him. Pres did a great selling job. I think he fooled my sister, as well."

"Maybe. Maybe not."

Alex narrowed his gaze at her. "How can you say that? She had to have fallen for his lies. Let's not forget that she's pregnant with his child and he is nowhere to be found."

"His shirts in the closet," Samantha said. "Your sister had to have seen them. I think she knows who he really is."

Alex looked stricken. "You're saying she was in on this deception?"

"I'm saying it's likely, given that Presley became Preston Wellington III about the time he met her."

"Exactly." Alex sighed. "Even if you're right, he could still be behind her hit-and-run."

She couldn't argue that.

"And how do you explain the man who's been following us. Or the attempt on our lives? Someone doesn't want us returning to Miami with what we know. Who else could it be besides Presley Wells?"

She wished she had an answer. But she knew C. B. Graham would never have accepted Presley Wells as a son-in-law if he knew about his background. Just as he would never accept Samantha Peters of Algona, Iowa, dirt-poor farm girl as a daughter-in-law.

"You all right?" Alex asked, his gaze softening with concern. He squeezed her hand gently. "Let's hope Presley is the man you thought he was. Believe me nothing would make me happier for my sister's sake." He leaned toward her, meeting her gaze as he leaned in to kiss her. The kiss was soft and gentle. Almost a goodbye kiss.

"Let's go see my sister."

ALEX WAS GLAD TO SEE that Caroline was awake and sitting up in bed when he and Samantha entered her room. She smiled and seemed happy to see them.

"Pres just called again," she said, her hand going to her stomach, her smile broadening.

"I'm sorry I missed that," Alex said.

Caroline's smile slipped a little. "You'll meet him soon enough."

"Oh? Is he on his way back?" Alex asked.

Caroline seemed to ignore his question as she turned to Samantha. "It is so good of you to stop by."

"How are you feeling?" Samantha asked, brushing Alex's hand as she stepped past him.

He moved to the end of the bed, telling himself to let Samantha handle this. She was much better at this kind of thing. That's right. She was an agent. How did he keep forgetting that?

His gaze settled on her as she visited with his sister and he felt his body heat with a desire he wondered if he could ever quench. Even a lifetime with that woman wouldn't be enough, he suspected.

Caroline seemed relieved to have Samantha there. "The doctor told me I was unconscious for a while. I'm so glad the baby is all right." She looked up and caught him watching Samantha. She quirked an eyebrow. "Has something been going on that I don't know about?" Her expression made it clear that she couldn't imagine a more unlikely pair.

"Alex?" Caroline's gaze seemed to take in Samantha's attire that he'd purchased for her in Tennessee, an admiring glance before she met his gaze again. "You both seem…different."

"We need to talk," Alex said, moving to the other side of his sister's bed. "And not just about me and Samantha."

He saw Samantha take Caroline's hand as if to protect her, to protect Presley.

"I went by your condo," Alex said.

Caroline's eyes widened. "Why?"

"Why do you think? You were unconscious. I wanted to find your fiancé and get him to the hospital."

Caroline said nothing, but seemed to stiffen as if bracing herself for the storm.

"You know Preston is really Presley Wells, don't you?" Samantha asked before Alex could.

Surprise, then resignation registered on his sister's face before being quickly replaced by a steely determination he knew only too well.

"We went to Tennessee," Alex said. "We know everything."

Not quite, but Samantha didn't correct him.

Caroline had closed her eyes. He could see that she was squeezing Samantha's hand. "Have you told Daddy?"

"I wouldn't do that."

Her eyes came open again.

"Tell me what's going on," Alex demanded.

"If you know everything then what is there to tell?"

"Where is your fiancé?"

His sister shook her head, tears brimming in her eyes.

All the anger seemed to rush out of him. He slumped on the edge of her bed. Then, as if on impulse, he leaned into Caroline and because of her broken arm and leg, gave her an awkward hug.

Caroline let go of Samantha's hand to wrap her arms around his neck. "Trust me," she whispered. "Everything is going to be fine." They stayed like that for a long moment.

He heard Samantha step out of the room to give them

some privacy. A moment later he heard the ring of her cell phone.

"Let me help you," Alex said to his sister as he pulled back from the hug.

"You already have. I'm glad you know about Presley. I tried to tell you the other day at Weddings Your Way, but I was afraid of your reaction."

"It isn't my reaction you have to worry about," he said.

"In time, Daddy will come around, you'll see." Caroline pressed his hand to her stomach. "You're going to love Presley." She smiled. "He reminds me of you."

WALKING DOWN THE HALL away from the two guards outside Caroline's room, Samantha took the call, glad to see it was Clare getting back to her.

"Are you sitting down?" Clare said.

"No, should I be?"

"Maybe. I did some checking on the names you gave me. I started with Alex Graham, since I knew you were in Tennessee with him and Rachel seemed to be worried about you."

Samantha held her breath.

"Financially solvent and then some. It doesn't look like he spends even the money he makes."

"What are you saying?"

"He's loaded and apparently has made some good investments. He could live much better than he does. From what I could find out, he lives in a small beach house, old neighborhood, though not a bad one."

Samantha felt a wave of relief. No red flags. Nothing to cause her concern. Maybe Alex Graham was just what he appeared to be. She sure hoped so because she was crazy about him. And it scared her half to death.

"Of course Alex doesn't have anything compared to his father," Clare continued. "Whew! Is C. B. Graham rich."

"Any recent big investments?"

"As a matter of fact…"

Just as Samantha had been led to believe, C. B. Graham had invested quite heavily with his future son-in-law, Pres. It wasn't enough to make a dent in his overall wealth, but it was substantial enough that it wouldn't go unnoticed if C.B. lost it.

"And Brian Graham?" Samantha asked, pretty sure he had invested, as well.

"No record of him investing any money with Wells," Clare said, surprising her. Samantha had been so sure. Brian had seemed awfully eager to find Pres. But maybe it had just been concern for his father.

"Probably didn't invest because he's in trouble financially," Clare said.

"What?" She remembered the cocky way Brian had been at the Holcom-Anders wedding. "But I thought he ran the Graham empire?"

"Not all of it. That kind of wealth is never all in one pot—or all under one control," Clare said. "But Brian Graham had been given a substantial amount of it to control it appears."

"And he's lost it?"

"No, but he's made some bad investments and unless he gets a windfall, he will have lost it all," Clare said.

Brian was in trouble financially? Did C.B. know? And what did that have to do with Presley? Everything, she thought. If Brian were desperate, would he invest in one of Presley's projects secretly as a last-ditch effort to save himself? It might explain why Brian was so anxious to find Presley.

She thanked Clare and closing her phone started back down the hall toward Caroline's room. A nurse Samantha had seen before came out of Craig Johnson's room just down the hall.

Samantha slowed to talk to her, the nurse smiling as she recognized her. "I saw you coming out of Craig Johnson's room. How is he doing?" In truth, she was surprised he was still in the hospital. Shouldn't he have been released by now?

The nurse's smile instantly faded. "I'm sorry, you must not have heard. He's in a coma."

"A coma?" But Samantha had been convinced there wasn't anything wrong with him. "I don't understand."

The nurse shook her head. "It happened about an hour ago. We found him on the floor. He'd obviously hit his head when he fell. No one knows what happened. Possibly some sort of seizure from his other ˌ ˌ ˌ ˌ during his attack."

Samantha had a pretty good idea she ˌ happened to Johnson. Whoever had tri ˌ before had been more successful this ˌ

"I saw that you were visiting Ms. Graham," the nurse said. "A lovely woman. I'm so happy for her and her fiancé. He obviously loves her so much."

Samantha came alert at the nurse's last remark. "You've seen him?"

The nurse realized her mistake at once but Samantha wasn't about to let the woman off the hook.

"It's all right. You can tell me," Samantha said. "I'll keep your confidence. He's been here?" She thought of Craig Johnson down the hall now in a coma. Was it possible Presley…

The nurse glanced around then leaned in conspiratorially. "He's been by every night."

The woman had to be mistaken. Samantha stared at her, trying to hide her surprise. "Ms. Graham's fiancé has been coming to see her every night?"

"Every night since the accident. The nights she was unconscious, I found him asleep in a chair next to her bed when I checked on her before the shift change."

"You're sure it was her fiancé?"

The nurse nodded and smiled. "Good-looking man with dark hair, pale blue eyes and a great smile."

That would be Presley. "And that's the only time he comes by to visit, at night?" Samantha asked keeping her voice down.

"Every night since she was admitted," the nurse said. "Sneaks in after visiting hours." She shrugged as if it was no big deal he was breaking the rules. "Leaves before dawn. I guess he has a job to get to.

He obviously is a workingman, you know, by the way he dresses."

Presley was working *something,* that was for sure. "What about the guard at her door?" Samantha asked.

The nurse looked sheepish. "We distract him."

Samantha groaned inwardly. What if the man the nurse had described had been a killer? Quite simply, Caroline Graham would be dead.

"I take it Ms. Graham is in on this?" Samantha asked, knowing that had to be the case.

The nurse grinned. "It is kind of romantic. Just seeing the two of them together. They are so much in love."

And in cahoots. But over what? Caroline had led them to believe that Pres was out of the country and still trying to get back to her.

The question was, why had she lied? None of this made any sense. Unless the nurse was mistaken and the man who was visiting Caroline each night wasn't Presley. Had Caroline found not just one but two men who were that good-looking and obviously charming, as well?

But the nurse had mentioned Presley's pale blue eyes and they *were* incredible. A cool-water blue accented by dark lashes. And when Presley smiled, it was quite re-markable. No, the man had to be Presley.

"It's that other man that we hate to see here," the nurse said, then seemed to regret having spoken out of turn.

"What man was that?" Samantha asked, her ears perking up.

"The brother. Not the nice one who's in there with her now but the other one."

Brian. "Has he visited much?"

"A couple of times with their father. Is he really as rich as everyone says?" She saw Samantha's expression. "Sorry. A few times he came by alone. He was fine when the father was with them but the other times he upset Ms. Graham and this last time—"

"When was that?"

"An hour or two ago," the nurse said, frowning as she looked at her watch. "I think he came about the time we were trying to revive Mr. Johnson. Anyway, I heard them arguing all the way down the hall and finally had to ask him to leave."

What had Brian been arguing with his sister about? Presley Wells no doubt.

A call bell rang at the nurses' station. The nurse excused herself and hustled down the hallway.

Samantha heard Alex come out of his sister's room and turned to look at him. He looked awful and the news she had to give him wasn't going to make him feel any better.

Chapter Sixteen

Alex raked a hand through his hair as he looked at Samantha. She looked as down as he felt. "Caroline's lying through her teeth."

Samantha nodded and motioned for him to follow her to the solarium. "Presley isn't out of the country," she said the moment they were alone. "He's been here every night, staying by your sister's bedside while she was unconscious."

Alex swore. "How—?"

"He's charmed the nurses into helping him sneak past the guards."

"We'll see about that." He started to storm past Samantha, planning to see that those nurses lost their jobs—along with the guards he'd hired.

"Wait," Samantha said, grabbing his arm. "You don't want to do that. Think about Caroline. Obviously Presley cares about her. Why else hang around here?"

He swore and walked to the sliding doors, shoving

them open to step out into the hot humid night air as he looked out at the city. What Samantha said made sense. Or did it? He stepped back into the air-conditioned room, closing the door behind him.

"Why *would* Presley hang around here, especially if I'm right and he's hoodwinked my family, stolen their money and planning to take off?"

"Exactly," Samantha said. "Maybe he did con your father and brother into investing with him. But he already has their money, right? What reason does he have to stick around but the fact that he loves your sister and can't leave her now?"

"He wants something."

"What?"

Alex shook his head. "Why sneak around the hospital at night? Why have Caroline and his office tell everyone he's not even in the country? He isn't done," Alex said as the theory began to grow. "He's waiting for something. Something he needs before he's done. Maybe one more big score."

"And how do you explain him coming to the hospital every night to be with Caroline?"

Alex looked up in surprise. "That's it. He needs whatever it is from Caroline." He glanced at his watch. "Presley comes by every night, right?"

She nodded.

"Then tonight we'll be ready for him." She started to object but he cut her off. "You have all those wonderful contacts. Can you get a video set up in my sister's room?

I'm sure we can get her out of the room long enough for your contacts to set up the equipment. Given what I have on that nurse I'm willing to bet she'll help us."

Samantha had the good sense not to argue. She got on her cell phone, turning away from him, as she made the arrangements. Clearly she thought the video would prove that Presley was just a man in love.

Alex was betting it was going to prove to be a lot more than that.

SAMANTHA GOT the technical team to come in and install the equipment while the nurse wheeled Caroline down the hall for what was supposed to be more X-rays.

Both Samantha and Alex stayed out of sight, wanting Caroline to believe they had left for the night. Samantha suspected that Caroline would call Presley when the coast was clear for him to return to the hospital.

She'd had the team set up a monitoring device so she and Alex would be able to not only see but hear everything that went on in Caroline's room. All they had to do was wait in the empty hospital room down the hall.

Alex was sprawled in one of the chairs next to Samantha, both of them facing the screen. Nothing had happened since the nurse had returned Caroline to her room. Samantha was beginning to think that Caroline had warned Presley not to come tonight.

Then, just past nine, Caroline checked her watch and made a call.

"Brian, I need to see you," she said, sounding more

upset than she appeared on the video screen. "Yes now. It can't wait. No, I can't talk about it on the phone. I have to see you. It's about Preston." She listened for a moment, then hung up and checked her watch before lying back in the bed and closing her eyes.

"What the hell?" Alex said.

Samantha was just as surprised as Alex by the call to Brian. "The nurse told me that Brian upset Caroline on his recent visit and they had to ask him to leave."

"Something's up," Alex said. "You saw the way she was acting."

Samantha nodded and they waited. Not twenty minutes later, Brian slipped into Caroline's room. Clearly, he had figured out a way to get past the nurse.

"So where is he?" Brian said without preamble once in Caroline's room.

She shook her head, tears filling her eyes. "I don't know. I just found out that he isn't even Preston Wellington III. His name is Presley Wells." She began to cry.

"I had no idea my sister was such a good actress," Alex said under his breath.

Brian swore as he moved to the bed and tossed his sister the box of tissues. "I already knew that. I thought you had some new information. You got me over here for this?"

"You knew?" Caroline cried. "Why didn't you tell me?"

Brian shook his head, looking more than a little upset. "I need to find this fiancé of yours. Do you understand?"

Samantha figured Caroline understood perfectly.

"Could you just hold me for a minute?" Caroline asked, still crying.

Brian looked as though he'd rather leap out the window but he awkwardly leaned over and put his arms around her.

Caroline put her arms inside his coat and pulled him closer, drawing back a couple of times to blow her nose, until Brian seemed to have had enough.

"Look, you got the family into this mess, Caroline, you have to help me find him. If he calls you, find out where he is. You owe me."

Caroline nodded, red-eyed and still weepy. "I'll do everything I can, Brian. I'm so sorry."

"Brian's actually buying her act," Alex said, sitting up and shaking his head in wonder.

As Brian left, Caroline shut down the waterworks instantly and reached beneath her covers to pull out a small object that Samantha recognized at once.

"She's got Brian's PDA."

Alex was up out of his seat and pacing the floor. "What the hell? You can bet Presley Wells is behind this."

But Samantha was thinking about what information Brian would have on his PDA—and what Alex had said about a last big score.

Presley showed up a little after eleven. It was all Alex could do not to storm down the hall and beat the hell out of him.

Instead, Samantha stayed between him and the door

just in case and he watched the monitor with her, pretty sure he knew what would happen next.

He watched Presley go to Caroline, hold her, kiss her, brush her hair back from her face, and felt uncomfortable witnessing something so personal and intimate.

Alex could feel Samantha's gaze on him. "Okay, maybe he loves her. Or maybe he's an even better actor than my sister."

He watched Presley Wells lean over Caroline as if to give her a kiss, his heart in his throat. If the man made any kind of move to hurt her—Presley pulled back.

Caroline was smiling up at her fiancé. It broke Alex's heart to see the love in her eyes. As Presley started to leave, she pulled him back as if somehow she knew she might never see him again. Alex saw fear in her face as Presley left. Then tears.

"Son of a bitch. She knows he's not coming back. I have to see her. Keep an eye on Presley but I think we both know where he's headed."

Caroline's eyes widened with fear when she saw Alex step into her room. "What are you doing here?" she asked, hurriedly drying her tears.

"I know Presley was just here. I know you gave him Brian's PDA. Caroline, why?"

"Alex, you don't understand. It isn't what you think."

"I know we sometimes do things when we're in love…"

She shook her head. "It isn't like that. Presley found out that Brian has been skimming money out of my trust fund. He needs to get into the records to prove it."

Alex shook his head sadly. "Caroline, don't you realize what you've done? He is going to clean out every dime and take off."

"You're wrong, Alex. He's trying to protect me, our family, our baby. He loves me. You'll see tonight, after he finds the evidence, you'll see that you're wrong about him."

Alex nodded, unable to argue anymore with his sister. She loved the man and was blind to what was happening. Later, Alex would come back because Caroline was going to need him. Arguing with her now wasn't going to make that easier for her later.

"Everything is going to be all right," he said.

"Presley knows what he's doing."

Alex didn't doubt that for a moment.

"Don't go after him," Caroline cried. "You don't realize how dangerous this is. Someone has been trying to hurt Presley."

Alex stopped at the door. "Caroline, someone tried to kill me and Samantha in Tennessee."

Shock registered on her face. "It wasn't Presley."

He gave her a sympathetic look. "I'll be back." Then he pushed out of the door, trying to ignore her cries for him to stop.

When Presley left he had Brian's PDA and it didn't take much to figure out where he was headed. To the Graham building headquarters and Brian's personal offices. No doubt Caroline had given him the codes to get in.

Both guards were at their posts again. Alex promised himself he would fire them both as soon as he returned.

Samantha was waiting for him downstairs. "He took a cab. I have the number."

Alex swore, finding it hard to believe that his sister would be taken in by this man. "Obviously, he's coerced Caroline into helping him rip off the family. Even love can be a form of coercion," he added, looking at Samantha.

"I like to believe love doesn't make you do things you don't want to do," Samantha said.

He met her gaze, the depth of his feelings for her convincing him that a person in love did a lot of things he wouldn't have conceived of just days before. He knew firsthand since the last person he wanted to be in love with was an agent. Especially right now.

Samantha started to reach for her cell phone but he placed a hand on her arm to stop her.

"Let me handle this," he said. "It's my *family*. Can you give me this? I know you're an agent. I've accepted that." Her look said she didn't believe it. He wasn't sure he did, either. "I have to handle this in a way that Caroline will be hurt the least. Do you understand?"

"You know I do."

"Then no agents. Just let me go alone."

"I can't do that, Alex. Maybe Presley's only crime was falling in love with a rich woman. Maybe it's swindling your family. But one of Weddings Your

Way's clients is still missing after her abduction in front of the shop. There still hasn't been a ransom demand. For all I know Presley is somehow connected to all of it. And if that's the case, I can't leave the agency out of it."

"But you can give me a little time," Alex said, knowing that he was using her feelings for him. Wasn't he just as bad as Presley? He saw the pain in her expression.

"I won't make the call *yet*," she said. "But don't try to stop me from coming with you."

"Would it do any good?"

She shook her head.

"That's what I thought."

"Let's take my car," Samantha said. "He doesn't know it." A set of car lights blinked in the lot.

The headlights Alex saw were connected to a sleek black sports car convertible, the top up. "That's yours? You had someone deliver it?" He couldn't help his surprise. But then how could he forget the body she'd been hiding under those baggy suits? Or the brain and determination of the woman she'd been hiding behind the role of wedding planner?

SAMANTHA TOSSED Alex the keys. He looked surprised, then grinned at her. All she could think about now was Presley. How could she have been so wrong about him? She hadn't stopped believing in him—even when all the evidence was so weighted against him. Until tonight.

Caroline had taken her brother's PDA. Unless Samantha missed her guess, it would contain passwords to Graham accounts. Presley could clean out whatever funds Brian managed for the family. Why else get Caroline to steal it for him?

"Ready?" Alex asked as he slid behind the wheel.

"You do know how to drive something other than a truck, don't you?"

He cranked up the engine. As it roared to life, he shot her a look. "What the hell's under that hood?"

She grinned back at him. "You're about to find out."

He hit the gas and they careened out of the parking lot. "I think in this we might be able to beat Presley to the Graham building."

Samantha nodded, her thoughts on what she'd agreed to do. She should have called Rachel. She should have had the team meet them. She'd broken one of the cardinal rules of Weddings Your Way. It might cost her her job.

But as she looked over at Alex, she also knew that he needed to do this on his own. The team was standing by. All she had to do was call them and they would be there in minutes. She could give Alex a little time. And it wasn't as if she was letting him go in alone.

"There is something you should know," she said as Alex took a corner. "Brian's in financial trouble. Possibly on the verge of losing everything your father entrusted to him."

Alex didn't ask how she knew this. He seemed to

remember who she was, what she was. His face clouded. "You're sure?"

She nodded. "So the only thing Presley can steal is the rest of Caroline's trust fund."

Alex seemed to concentrate on his driving without looking at her. "Do you have any idea what my father is going to do when he hears about this? How much did my father invest with Presley?"

"A lot, but," she added quickly, "not enough to jeopardize the family fortune."

"And Brian. He invested, too, right?"

"Apparently not. At least not on paper."

Alex let out a low whistle. "What about Caroline and Presley?"

She hesitated. "They both sank most everything into this condominium project near the water."

"Presley had some money?" Alex asked, sounding surprised.

"Some. Not as much as Caroline of course."

"You think Brian invested with Presley under the table knowing how risky it was. Maybe made a deal to bring our father into it to sweeten the pot. That would be like Brian. So Brian lied to C.B. about how risky the venture was. He put his head on the chopping block and now Presley is about to chop it off."

That did seem to be the case. Samantha watched Miami became a blur as Alex drove toward the Graham building. "But if Presley had it all working for him, why try to kill us?" she asked, thinking aloud.

"Because he couldn't let us return from Tennessee and tell Brian and C.B. who he really was before he finished whatever it is he's doing tonight," Alex said.

Maybe. Samantha was still having trouble believing it. "Why tonight? Why not a month ago?"

Alex cocked his head at her, his smile heart-stopping. "I'll ask him when I see him."

She leaned back in the seat unable not to think about Caroline and Presley. No more an unlikely match than she and Alex. C.B. would do everything possible to prevent Caroline from marrying Presley even if it turned out that his only crime was lying about his background—and possibly losing Graham money in one of his schemes.

She glanced over at Alex. He was already the black sheep of the family. Imagine how C.B. would react if he knew about her and Alex. If C.B. knew about her past. It wasn't as if a person could keep something like that a secret. Hadn't Caroline and Presley known that?

"You know my whole life history," she said. "But I don't know anything about you."

"Your whole life history?" He chuckled as he was forced to stop for a light. "Not likely. You know as much about me as I do you."

She shook her head. "I told you why there was no man in my life."

The light changed. Alex seemed to concentrate harder on his driving. A muscle jumped in his jaw. "You and I have both been hiding. The last woman I trusted proved to want nothing more than my money. I guess I've always had a hard time believing a woman could love me for anything but my money." He shot her a glance. "Once they hear the Graham name…"

Samantha smiled ruefully and nodded. "The exact opposite of Presley Wells."

Alex's lips turned up at little. "At least he knows Caroline loves him for who he is. Or did."

Ahead, the Graham office building loomed up into the Miami sky.

"This car, it's the part of you that I'm just getting to know, isn't it?" Alex said, his face serious as he parked and shut off the engine.

"Yes." She felt his gaze flick over her as they both exited the car and headed for the security entrance. The question was: was Alex Graham man enough to handle that woman? At least that was the question she imagined he was asking himself.

Samantha on the other hand had been convinced a long time ago that Alex Graham was plenty man enough for both of her lives.

In the end, he would have to make that decision. Whether or not he could live with her being an agent.

Or she would be faced with her own decision. Could she live without Alex Graham?

Samantha glanced back at the street and saw a tan sedan drive slowly by. They'd been followed from the hospital. She reached into her purse, her hand closing on her gun as Alex put in a call to his father.

"I need the code to get into the Graham building," he said into his cell while Samantha watched the street. "There isn't time to explain. For once, Dad, just don't fight me. Give me the code *now*."

Alex listened, then pressed the key pad. The door opened and he ran toward the stairs, Samantha right behind him. The door thunked shut as a set of headlights swung past, reflecting in the window in the door.

"Dad, I have to go. I don't care if you call Brian. I figured you would the moment you hang up anyway," Alex said into the phone. "But when you do, ask him where his PDA is." He closed his phone and pressed his back against the wall of the stairwell next to her.

Samantha heard the outer door open and close. A moment later the elevator doors hummed open. She waited next to Alex until she heard them close and the elevator begin its ascent.

Pushing open the stairwell door, she looked up to see what floor Presley got off on. Fourth.

Behind her, she heard Alex already running up the stairs to the fourth floor.

Chapter Seventeen

Samantha caught up to him. Alex was trying to open one of the doors. "Here, let me," she said, stepping past him and pulling out her kit.

"How could I forget you have a talent for breaking into places?" he said stepping aside.

Yes, she thought, meeting his gaze. How could he forget? She felt her heart ache. He *couldn't* forget. Any more than he could forget what she did for a living and it wasn't the wedding planning part that she feared he couldn't live with.

"Shh," Alex said. "He's coming this way."

She got the door open. "In here." But when she turned, Alex was gone. Damn him. Where had he gone? She could hear footfalls. Presley was headed in her direction. Quickly, she ducked into the room and looked for a place to hide.

If she was right about why he'd had Caroline take Brian's PDA, then Presley would head for the computer.

She ducked behind one of the large overstuffed leather chairs off to one side of the desk and waited.

The door creaked open. Footfalls headed for the desk. She heard the squeak of the office chair as someone sat down. Cautiously, she peeked out. From where she hid, she could see the backside of a man's head but there was no mistaking who it was. Presley Wells aka Preston Wellington III.

Samantha wondered where Alex had gone. She just hoped he stayed put. She needed to get Presley with the evidence, otherwise all they had on him was trespassing. From what Clare had been able to find out, the money Presley had taken from C. B. Graham was for a legitimate investment.

She waited, her heart in her throat as she watched Presley search Brian's PDA until he found what he was looking for, then turned to the computer to key in the passwords.

Somewhere in the building she heard a door slam. Presley heard it, too. He began to work faster and in a few moments she heard a pleased sound come from him, then pages began to come out of the laser printer.

Presley stood and went to the printer, his back to her. She drew the gun from her purse but didn't rise. Not yet. Just a few more moments and he would have the evidence on him. The printer stopped. She saw him pick up the sheets of paper, fold them and start to put them in his breast pocket. Samantha made her move.

VICTOR CONSTANTINE loved the element of surprise. But wasn't wild about being surprised.

Unfortunately, upon his return from Tennessee, he'd gone straight from the airport to the hospital only to find Alex Graham's pickup parked in the lot. How was that possible? He'd been so certain Alex Graham was dead.

He quickly realized that he'd failed in Tennessee. There was some irony to the fact, given that his client had failed to put the payment in his account. It almost balanced things out. Almost.

Victor wished he could call the client and give him the news. Except the client had gotten rid of the cell phone thinking that would be the end of it.

Victor had little to go on. Just the sound of the man's voice—and now Alex Graham and Samantha Peters. Victor had planned on using the woman Alex Graham and Samantha Peters had visited at the hospital—Caroline Graham. But now that wouldn't be necessary. He waited in the darkness outside the hospital. Something told him that the pair would lead him to his client. Or the client would find them. Either way worked.

It didn't take that long before Alex Graham and Samantha Peters emerged, jumped into her little black number and sped off with Alex driving. Victor was right behind.

Then he'd had a stroke of good luck. As he'd watched the two enter the high-rise office building, he'd decided to wait. Within two minutes a taxi arrived and dropped off a dark-haired young man.

Victor had his window down and was parked where he could hear the man talking to the taxi driver. Wrong voice. Not his client.

Victor started to get out of his car and follow the man but another car had pulled up, the driver watching the exchange between the taxi driver and the man with almost as much interest as Victor.

As the dark-haired man disappeared into the building, the other man followed, giving an order to his driver to wait. Victor would have known that voice anywhere. But it was the way the man ordered the driver to wait that cinched it.

Victor quickly got out of his car and hurried after his client, catching up to him just as he opened the office building door. The surprise on the man's face was priceless as Victor locked an arm around the man's throat and forced him inside the building. Victor wanted to hurt him right then and there, but he was nothing if not pragmatic.

"You owe me money," he whispered into the man's ear. "Quite a lot of money."

Recognition shone in the man's terrified eyes, then angry arrogance. "You bungled the job. You didn't kill them. I owe you nothing."

Victor tightened his hold on the man's throat. "The money or I will kill you here."

An unintelligible sound came out of his client. Victor, who had made few mistakes in his life, loosened his hold. Pop. Pop. Instantly he recognized the sound of bullets passing through a small caliber gun's silencer. It took a little longer to feel the pain.

Victor staggered as his client broke away turning to fire once more before disappearing into the elevator. Clutching his side, Victor slumped to the floor. He could only watch as the elevator doors closed. His pained gaze went to the numbers lighting up above the closed elevator doors.

It wasn't until the light stopped at 4 that Victor forced himself to his feet.

ALEX COULD SEE Presley in Brian's office but he couldn't be sure where Samantha had gone. He stayed back in the shadows watching Presley at the computer, then at the printer. Where the hell was Samantha?

He heard the elevator doors open down the hall. Someone else in the building? His father? Or Brian? Or both? Alex knew he had to make a move as he saw that Presley had heard the elevator doors and knew someone was coming, as well.

Crouching down, Alex readied himself for when Presley came out the office door. He'd jump him and pray the man didn't have a gun.

But after a moment, Alex realized his mistake. He peeked through the office window. No Presley. And yet he hadn't come out this door.

While Alex had forgotten about it, Presley obviously had known about the secret panel that opened between Brian's office and the one next door. Where the hell was he now?

No Samantha, either.

Nor, he realized, did he hear anyone down the hall. And yet someone had gotten off the elevator.

With a curse, he realized that they had all gone through the back way into Brian's private inner office.

Alex reached for the doorknob. It refused to turn. He was locked out. But what scared him most was that Samantha was locked inside. Somewhere. Agent or not, she was in danger. Maybe more danger than she knew because she still wanted to believe in Presley Wells's innocence.

SAMANTHA HAD BEEN ready to take Presley Wells down. Like Alex, she had expected him to head for the main office door which would have given her time to come out from behind the chair, aim the weapon and take him by surprise.

Instead, he had touched a panel on the wall next to the printer and then melted into the opening that suddenly appeared, leaving her two steps behind.

Just seconds before that, she'd heard the elevator doors down the hall, heard footfalls. More than one set.

She hurried over to the panel that had closed behind Presley and felt on the wall where she'd seen him do the same. The panel slid open soundlessly and she stepped into the cool darkness, her gun raised.

She heard voices somewhere in front of her. Then a pop followed by a crash. Her heart in her throat, she hurried forward, leading with her weapon.

The first thing she saw was the body on the floor. "Presley?" As she stepped forward she saw that the man wore a pair of dark chinos and a polo shirt. Presley had been dressed in a work shirt, jeans and denim jacket.

As she moved to see the face of the man on the floor, she heard a sound behind her. Just as she recognized Brian Graham sprawled facedown, she was jumped from behind. A strong hand wrestled the gun from her fingers and shoved her. She stumbled and almost fell over Brian on the floor.

Turning back toward the darkness of another adjoining office, she saw Presley. He held her gun in his hand as he locked the door behind them. "So you know who I am."

She stepped back, bumping into the desk. She pretended to use both hands to brace herself on the desk, while she mentally tried to remember if she'd seen anything within reach that she could use as a weapon.

"Easy," Presley said. "Let's not do anything crazy, okay?" His voice had the same gentle, slightly Southern drawl she remembered. He had another weapon stuck in the waistband of his jeans. This one had a silencer on it and she knew it was what she'd heard just moments before.

"You shot Brian?"

"Actually, he tried to shoot *me*," Presley said. "You don't believe me." He stepped closer. "I love Caroline. But I think you know that."

Surprisingly, she believed him. She did know. "So this is just about money."

"Just about money?" He laughed. "You and I both know people have killed for less."

"Do you really think you can get away with this?"

"For Caroline's sake and our baby's, I sure hope so."

Brian stirred on the floor, groaning as he worked his way into a sitting position, his back against the wall.

Presley hadn't pointed her gun at her. But although he held it pointed downward, it wouldn't take much for him to raise it and fire at either her or Brian.

"I have proof what Brian was up to." Presley patted the breast pocket of his jacket.

Brian swore. "He's lying. He's a con man. His name is Presley Wells. He's here to clean out my accounts."

Presley let out a humorless laugh. "I would be too late for that. The accounts have already been emptied. I would imagine Caroline's trust fund is also empty. Caroline thought she got away with your PDA clean but you were on to us, weren't you?"

"What is going on?" Samantha demanded, looking from one man to the other but all the time worrying about where Alex was. And what he would do next.

"Brian discovered who I really was and came to me with a deal," Presley said. "A scam to bilk his father out of more money. Brian said he had an investment that was too good to pass up, but risky. His father would never go for it. Unless it looked like it came from me. C.B. liked me. Of course C.B. wouldn't go for it unless Brian gave his stamp of approval."

"Don't listen to him," Brian said rubbing the side of

his head where Presley must have hit him. Samantha couldn't tell if Brian was really hurt or just biding his time, waiting for Presley to let his guard down.

"If all this is true, then why didn't you go to C.B. with it?" she asked Presley.

This time his laugh was sincere. "Brian would have told him the truth about my…background and then who do you think C.B. would have believed? So I went along with it, pretending I was in it for the money."

"Like this isn't about money," Brian piped up. "You think anyone is going to believe your story? Your word against mine. There is no evidence that I was in on any of this."

Presley smiled and shook his head. "No, you made sure you'd covered your tracks. But the only reason I went along with your so-called deal was that I'd discovered you'd been siphoning off Caroline's trust fund account. I couldn't prove it. Until tonight. I found what I needed to put the nail in your coffin. I found proof that you made an attempt to pay a hired killer to get rid of me." He patted the papers in his pocket.

Brian, Samantha noticed, looked worried. "There isn't any…" His voice trailed off as if he'd just remembered something he'd overlooked.

Samantha jumped at the sound of a loud boom just outside the office door as if the door had been rammed by something heavy.

"No!" Samantha cried as she saw Brian launch himself at Presley. Presley raised her gun as if to fire, but it was knocked from his hand as a man came barreling into the room.

She caught only a glimpse of the man but she recognized his size and shape. The man who'd been following her and Alex? The hired assassin who'd tried to kill them in Tennessee?

"You think you can double-cross me?" the big man bellowed at Brian. "Are you crazy?"

Brian grabbed her fallen gun and pointed it at the man and yelled, "You're fired!"

Two explosions boomed in the office. Two quick shots. Brian's shot went wild, burrowing into the wall over the big man's head. Samantha wrested the other gun from Presley and fired. Hitting the big man in the leg.

But he didn't go down.

"Drop your gun! FBI!" she yelled, the gun aimed at the big man. "Drop your gun!"

Out of the corner of her eye, she saw Alex. He had something in his hands. A fire extinguisher.

The big man hadn't seen Alex but her biggest fear was that he would. As the man started to turn, Samantha's finger twitched on the trigger.

The man swung around. Samantha fired but the bullet that buried itself in his chest seemed to have no effect. The big man raised his gun, pointing it at Brian. "I always finish what I started."

Alex swung the fire extinguisher. It made a loud crack as it struck the big man's skull. Presley charged the big man, stepping into Samantha's line of fire.

Samantha shoved Presley aside, but not before the big man got off two shots. Alex swung the fire extinguisher again, this time the sound more of a sickening thunk followed by the heavy thud of a body hitting the floor.

"Bri, oh hell, Bri," she heard Alex saying as he bent over his brother.

Samantha was moving, first making sure that Presley hadn't been hit, then kicking the big man's gun out of his reach just in case he wasn't dead. But when she checked, she found he wasn't breathing.

She could hear sirens in the distance. Alex didn't seem to hear them, didn't seem to notice as he stripped off his shirt and pressed it to Brian's gaping chest wound.

She'd called the team against Alex's wishes. She'd had to. She hoped some day he would understand. Unfortunately everything had happened too fast. The team hadn't had time to get there. Maybe things would have gone differently. Or maybe not, she thought, looking down at Brian.

Brian was lying on the floor sobbing, his words barely audible. "I'm sorry. I just lost control of everything. I didn't know what to do. I had to stop Dad from finding out." He looked into Alex's face. "Everything just got out of control, you know?"

"Yeah, bro, I know," Alex said.

Samantha knew. She looked around the room. Presley was sitting on the floor looking sick, as if this wasn't what he'd wanted to happen, even though Brian had paid the big man on the floor to kill him. To kill all three of them.

"Don't tell Dad what I did," Brian said. "Promise me, you won't tell Dad."

"I promise," Alex said. But even as he said the words, Brian's eyes dimmed then went blank. His hand dropped from his chest. Alex let go of the shirt he'd pressed to the wound, then reached up gently and closed Brian's eyes.

When he looked over at Samantha, his gaze was filled with pain. Slowly, he rose and stepped to her. She felt a surge of warmth flow through her as he pulled her into his arms.

"Thank God, you're safe," Alex said against her hair. "Thank God."

Epilogue

"I still can't believe this," C. B. Graham grumbled as he reached for his drink on the table beside his chair.

Alex saw that his father had aged. C.B. seemed smaller, frailer, definitely chastened. C.B. had put all his money on Brian, so to speak. And Brian had caved under the strain.

"Go ahead and say it. I know what you're thinking. That I put too much pressure on my children. That I'm responsible for everything." C.B. stared down at his drink. "That if I'd been a better father…" His voice trailed off as he looked up at Alex, tears in his eyes. "I could have lost you all."

Brian had gotten in too deep, come up with a scheme to cover it up and involved Presley. Because of his background, Presley had felt he had to find proof against Brian before he could go to anyone with what he suspected.

"I still can't believe Brian hired a killer." C.B.'s voice

faltered. He swallowed and gripped his glass for a moment before taking a drink.

Alex glanced out the window. It had gotten dark and now all the lights in the garden twinkled. From somewhere, he heard music. The house felt alive again with Caroline back home.

"There's been enough blame," he said "Caroline is doing great. The doctor said her recovery is going well, she'll be back on her feet in no time."

C.B. nodded. "It's nice having her here." At her father's request, Caroline had agreed to recuperate at the house—but only if Presley would be allowed to move in, too.

"I want you to get to know him," Caroline had told C.B. "That's the deal. Take it or leave it."

C.B. had grudgingly taken it.

"She's going to marry that man, isn't she," he said now.

Alex nodded, smiling a little as he thought of his sister's fiancé. Caroline had been right. Alex liked Presley. Alex just wished his sister and Presley had trusted him enough to come to him when they'd suspected what Brian was up to.

But Samantha had taught him to put the past behind him. He couldn't change what had happened. All he could do now was look to the future. And what a future it could be.

"Presley reminds me of you," C.B. said and took a swallow of his drink.

Alex looked at his father, not sure what to say. As C.B. looked up from his glass, Alex felt the full weight of the old man's gaze. "I know I let you down when I wasn't interested in taking over the family business…"

"No, not that," C.B. said with a wave of his hand. "You and Presley, you're both stubborn, pigheaded and have to do everything your own way. Invariably the hard way."

The last thing Alex wanted to do was argue with his father. "If that's supposed to be a compliment, it's not coming off as one."

His father laughed, a wonderful sound after all pain they'd been through. "I'm trying to tell you that I admire you."

Alex stared at his father.

"The truth is you always were so damned much like me."

"Thank you," Alex said uncertainly.

C.B. laughed. "That definitely wasn't a compliment." But the pride he heard in his father's voice made him ache.

He looked at his father and saw something he'd missed for years. Grudging respect.

Is this what Brian had seen? Is this why Alex and Brian had never gotten along? Brian had tried so hard to please their father. While Alex hadn't tried at all for his father's respect or love, Brian had tried too hard. Brian had risked everything for it—and lost it all. How sad that Alex hadn't seen how much Brian had been struggling with that insecurity until after his brother's death.

While it had been Brian's scheme, Presley had

invested the money he'd received from both Brian and
C.B. and invested it in his companies. C.B. was going
to make a sizable sum. Brian would have, too, had he
lived.

Brian had been buried in the family cemetery on
the property. Most of what had really happened
had never surfaced. Not much of an investigation
followed the shootings. Alex knew he had Samantha
to thank for that. The police had just been happy to
finally have the notorious Victor Constantine and the
impeccable records of his kills. Looking for Constantine's clients would keep them busy for years.

There was a tap at the door. "Am I interrupting?"

Alex motioned Samantha into the room. C.B. lit up
at the sight of her. She went straight to the old man and
gave him a kiss on the cheek, then came over to settle
into the seat next to Alex. He couldn't believe what just
seeing her did to him.

"How's my favorite wedding planner?" C.B. asked,
all smiles now.

"Just fine." She glanced at Alex. He gave her hand
a squeeze.

Alex had realized something over the last week.
Samantha was her own woman. And that was what had
made him fall in love with her. He knew now that he
wouldn't have tried to change her for anything in the
world. He loved her and while her "second" job might
scare him, he had every faith in her abilities. Just as she
did in his.

"I was upstairs talking to Caroline and Presley about their wedding," Samantha said.

C.B. frowned. He'd come a long way over the last week, but he was still a curmudgeon at heart. He still wanted his only daughter to marry another blue blood.

"They've decided to postpone it until Caroline can walk down the aisle," Samantha said.

"If she waits too long, she'll have the baby in the middle of the aisle," Alex joked, excited about being an uncle. Even more excited about someday being a father. "You'll have to plan a joint wedding-baby shower."

Samantha jabbed him in the ribs with her elbow.

"I guess there is no talking her out of it," C.B. said and took a drink, but Alex could hear more than acceptance in his father's tone. "Well, there is the baby and Caroline obviously loves the man. Presley does seem to be good with money and it will be my first grandchild."

Alex smiled to himself, seeing his father's delight at being a grandfather. C.B., he thought, just might make a wonderful grandfather.

The door opened and Presley Wells stepped in with a roll of paper.

"Pres," his father said. The two men looked at each other, mutual acceptance and admiration growing between them. Presley Wells was the last man C.B. had wanted for his only daughter. And yet that was the man she'd chosen.

The fact that C.B. had let Presley move into the house with them said it all. Yes, Alex thought, his father was learning the fine art of compromise. It was something to see.

"That the condo project you've got there?" his father asked Presley.

"I'm thinking of making a few changes," Presley said, spreading out the plans on the table as he sat down across from C.B. "Want to take a look and see what you think?"

It was just a matter of time, Alex thought watching the two of them, before Presley Wells would be running the Graham empire.

Alex saw his chance to escape and slipped out of the den with Samantha in tow. They ran across the courtyard at the back of the house, laughing and falling into each others arms. They'd had so little time to be entirely alone over the past week.

But they were alone now and Alex planned to make the most of it. The night was warm, the garden lush. Lights flickered overhead. He could hear the soft murmur of the waterfalls, the gentle splash. The air was scented with the perfume of many flowers now in bloom. Everything couldn't have been more perfect.

"It is so beautiful here," she said as she turned to look out over the gardens.

He wrapped his arms around her, never wanting to let her go. And to think there'd been a time when he'd thought he'd never be able live with the fact that she was an agent.

But they both had dangerous jobs that they loved. They'd both chosen their own paths in life. And those paths had led them to each other.

Love, he realized, could conquer all.

Samantha snuggled against him, filled with a sense of joy at just being in his arms. His mouth felt warm as he nuzzled her neck, his breath tickling her skin. She felt safe. She felt loved. There was no greater feeling, she thought, as he drew her closer and they looked out on the gardens and the night.

They'd been through so much but it seemed to have made them stronger. It had definitely brought them closer.

Now if only there could be a break in the Sonya Botero kidnapping. The team was still investigating every avenue, following up on every lead, but still no word. Every day, they waited for the kidnappers to contact either Sonya's father or her fiancé, Juan. But still nothing.

Samantha wasn't giving up and neither was the team. She would just work harder on the case, praying there would be a break. Praying Sonya was still alive.

"Samantha?" Alex turned her slowly in his arms to face him. She looked up into his eyes and felt her heart begin to pound as his mouth dropped to hers in a soft sweet kiss. Then he drew her back to look at her.

She'd changed so much since she'd met him. She no longer wore the boxy suits. She no longer hid from her past or the girl she'd been. With Alex, she felt beautiful.

Presley Wells, for all the mistakes he'd made in investigating Brian by himself, had proven to her that there were men in the universe who were good and loyal and worth loving. And Alex Graham was one of them.

"Do you hear that?" Alex asked cocking his head and grinning as he drew her closer. Music moved on the breeze from the open terrace doors.

She smiled up at him as he pulled her into a slow dance, their bodies fitting together perfectly. She could feel the beat of his heart against her breast, hear his breath quickening as she touched her lips to his warm flesh just above his shirt collar.

The song ended and she realized that he'd danced her over to a stone bench beside a fountain. Caroline said the house should be filled with flowers and music and love.

Samantha couldn't agree more. Otherwise a house was nothing but an empty shell. Just as her heart had been before Alex.

Alex. He brushed a kiss over her lips. She breathed in his scents mingling with the fragrance of the garden, the water of the fountain, the uniquely south Florida smells. The night felt magical.

Her heart began to beat a little faster as he gently lowered her to the bench. And just like in the movies, he dropped to one knee in front of her, his eyes locking with hers.

"Samantha Peters, wedding planner and secret agent, will you marry me?" he asked, his gaze never leaving hers.

She swallowed, tears welling in her eyes as she smiled at him. "Oh, Alex."

From his pocket, he pulled out a small black box and held it out to her. Her fingers shook as she opened it and saw the diamond ring nestled in velvet.

"I never dreamed I could be this happy," she said, tears burning her eyes.

"Should I take that as a yes?"

"Oh, yes!"

He laughed, took the ring and placed it on her finger. She looked down at it, then up at him. The next thing she knew they were in each other's arms, holding each other tightly as if neither ever wanted to let go. She knew he had to be thinking about how close they'd come to losing each other.

Both knew because of their jobs, it could happen again. They'd made a silent pact to live every day as if there was no tomorrow.

"You know my father is going to want us to have a big wedding here," he said.

She smiled and tilted her head. "Would you hate that so much?"

He laughed. "Yes, but I'd do it for you. For my father." His eyes locked with hers, his bright in the twinkling lights that Caroline had asked to be strung in the trees of the garden the day she moved back in.

"My secret weapon soon-to-be spouse," he whispered. He said it with a kind of awe.

"You didn't tell your father, did you?"

"About your secret life?" Alex smiled and shook his

head. "He's only just accepted the fact that I'm a fireman. Anyway, I don't think his heart could take it."

She laughed softly, smiling as she cupped his jaw with her palm and looked into those wonderful eyes of his.

Alex pulled her closer. "There are some things, sweetheart, that should be our little secrets."

* * * * *

Don't miss the continuing saga of
MIAMI CONFIDENTIAL
and their search for Sonya Botero.
Automatic Proposal *by Kelsey Roberts*
is available in October 2007, only from Intrigue.

FREE!

4 Books
and a surprise gift!

We would like to take this opportunity to thank you for reading this Mills & Boon® book by offering you the chance to take FOUR more specially sele...

offer...

Acc...
you...
com...
You...

YES! that unless you hear from me. I will receive 6 superb new titles every month for just £3.10 each, postage and packing free. I am under no obligation to purchase any books and may cancel my subscription at any time. The free books and gift will be mine to keep in any case.

Ms/Mrs/Miss/Mr ....Initials.........................

17ZEF

BLOCK CAPITALS PLEASE

Surname ....

Address...

....Postcode ....

Send this whole page to:
UK: FREEPOST CN81, Croydon, CR9 3WZ